COOKIN' FOR BOB

COOKIN' FOR BOB

Cookin For Bob
Written by Pam Wingo and Linda Cash
Illustrations by Pam Wingo

Copyright © 2007
First Edition – First Printing December 2007
Library of Congress Number TXu1-363-142

ISBN # 978-1-934615-08-9
            1-934615-08-0

Published by Main Street Publishing, Inc., Jackson, TN.
Copy Editing by Shari B Hill
Edited by Sheri Isbell
Cover Design by Pam Wingo, Linda Cash and Shari B Hill
Printed and bound by NetPub, Poughkeepsie, NY.

For more information write Main Street Publishing, Inc.,
206 East Main St., Suite 207, P.O. Box 696, Jackson, TN 38302
Phone 1-731-427-7379 or toll free 1-866-457-7379.
E-mail:words@mspbooks.com for managing editor and mspsupport@charterinternet.com for customer service.
Visit us at   www.mainstreetpublishing.com and www.mspbooks.com.

MANY THANKS TO
BUCK FOR ALL HIS ENCOURAGEMENT,
OUR CHILDREN:
SAM AND ASHLEY
JASON, TRACIE, AND CANDY
FOR PUTTIN' UP WITH US AND ALL BOB'S SHENANIGANS,
DONNA FOR HER COMPUTER EXPERTISE.

AND OF COURSE...WE CAN'T LEAVE OUT ALL THE BOBS OF THE WORLD;
THANKS FOR THE MANY EXPERIENCES...IT'S BEEN LOVELY!!!

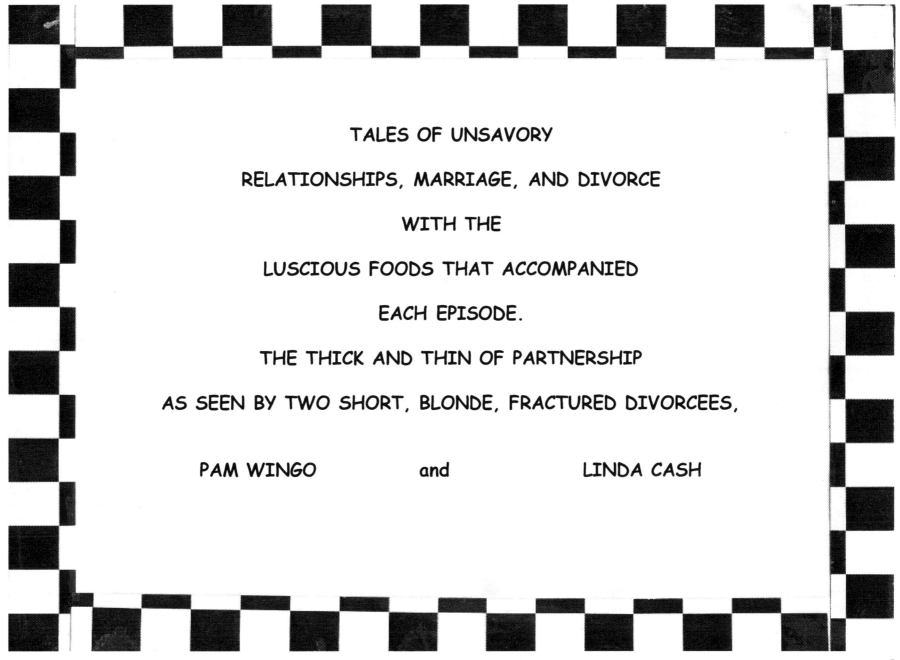

TALES OF UNSAVORY

RELATIONSHIPS, MARRIAGE, AND DIVORCE

WITH THE

LUSCIOUS FOODS THAT ACCOMPANIED

EACH EPISODE.

THE THICK AND THIN OF PARTNERSHIP

AS SEEN BY TWO SHORT, BLONDE, FRACTURED DIVORCEES,

PAM WINGO   and   LINDA CASH

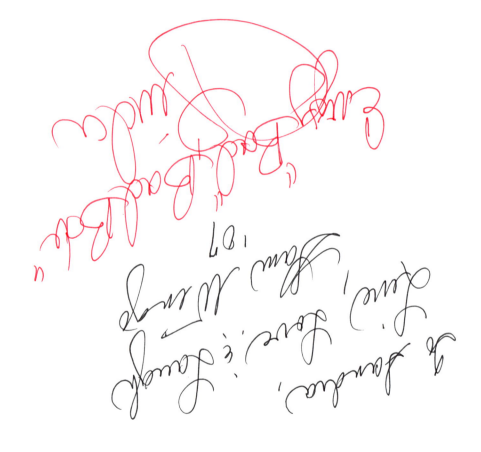

COOKIN' FOR BOB

COOKIN' FOR BOB

AN INTRODUCTION

Food, glorious food, the sustenance of Life!
Divorce, tragic divorce, the frustration of Life!
Marriage, illustrious marriage.........T.S. Eliot describes marriage as, "a dignified and commodious sacrament." While Shakespeare portrays it as, "a world-without-end bargain." WE WERE DEFINITELY NOT SHOPPING AT THE SAME STORE!!!!!

If you have ever been involved in a shaky hookup, YOU KNOW IT IS A LIVING HELL!!!!! When two people become bonded, no one bothers to mention possible side effects that may occur. Would they listen anyway?
Do these symptoms sound familiar?

Fatigue	Headaches	Nausea
Stomach Pain	Nose Bleed	Sore Throat
Dry Mouth	Loss of Appetite	Urinary Retention
Chest Pain	Irregular Heartbeat	Rash
Itching	Swelling	Dizziness
Trouble Breathing	Diarrhea	Confusion
Involuntary Muscle Movement		Changes in Mental Status

If these symptoms do not improve or they get worse...CONTACT YOUR LAWYER IMMEDIATELY!

Everybody's 'take' on a BAD attachment is different. We ALL think our situation is unique. And, in some ways it is, BUT, most of the characteristics of a marriage or relationship-gone-sour are the same. Trust us, we know your grief ALL TOO WELL, we've been there every step of the way! It's taken us years to lighten our load and LAUGH rather than cry. We are not making light of anyones misfortune, we have;

cried so much we've thought our eyeballs were fallin' out.
thought we were gonna die a thousand times.
anguished over so much, we have ulcers.

been so lonely, sad, and depressed we thought we could never leave the house,
much less the comforts of our beds, where we ate, read, moaned, paid bills.

The humiliation was debilitating! The pains were excruciating! It was a REAL catastrophe and often a present danger to all concerned, except for BOB, of course.

However, nothing stays the same. It is a new world everyday...thank you GOD! We just wish we had realized this earlier in life! AND, THIS IS WHAT WE WANT YOU TO DO...LAUGH, LAUGH, LAUGH. You are gonna make it! There are times we didnt think we would...BUT, HERE WE ARE AND YOU WILL SURVIVE TOO!!! Laughing your blues away!

Why a cookbook??? When we were growin' up, EVERYTHING went with music. You remembered everything with the memory of some song or some melody. You began to expect music to come out of nowhere when something happened! As we reflect back to OUR 'Gone Bad' relationships, it was not beautiful music we remembered.....it was what we were COOKIN' for BOB that made a lasting impression. So.....remember.....
this is no dress rehearsal...get out your POTS and PANS and let's live. LET'S GET GOIN'!!!

We have written a delightful, educational, in more ways than one, cookbook for those who have come to a parting of the ways...untied the knot. We hope you will enjoy our attempt to turn one of life's tragedies into a witty repertoire of stories and recipes that will heal a broken heart or soften a hard one, no pun intended, well, maybe just a small one.

ONLY THE NAMES HAVE BEEN CHANGED TO PROTECT THE GUILTY.

COOKIN' FOR BOB
by
PAM WINGO   and   LINDA CASH

STORIES AND RECIPES FOR:

A BABY BLUE POKER NIGHT

The poker group Money Bags Bob belonged to was meeting on its regular Tuesday night in our basement. Of course I was told by Bob to 'fix something really special' for what I called the local hard rollers. Just call me Blondie, 'cause for two day I had been runnin' around in my Baby Blue Ford Convertible with the White Top, gatherin' goodies to make my famous eggplant lasagna. But no matter how stupid, I just loved driving around in my beautiful car, particularly since I had bought it with my first teaching paycheck. It was soooooo cool and I was soooooo proud of myself and my fantastic down-topper.

After fixin' a beautiful spread and making sure everything was just right, I heard money jingling down the driveway. I knew right then it was time to exit! I said my hellos, got my nasty, big wet kisses, and quickly retreated upstairs. Sleep came easy even with all the laughter and what I assumed really bad jokes.

With dawns early light I woke to a horrible mess, stifling cigar odor, and OH MY GOSH, NO BABY BLUE CONVERTIBLE WITH THE WHITE TOP!!!!! Sitting in its place in the driveway was an ugly, very small, two door, dark blue, stick shift GREMLIN!!!!!

BOBSTER HAD LOST MY CAR IN THE POKER GAME!!!!!

TIP: If you can afford your own Baby Blue, you can afford to live on your own!
By damn, let the jackasses eat cake, if there is a next time!!!! Sorry donkeys, don't mean to insult ya'll.

RECIPES FOR:
Alcaponi Antipasta
Hardroller Eggplant Lasagna
Italian MEATBALLS in Marinara Sauce
Crusty Loaf Bread with Virgin Olive Oil
PW

PokHer Salad
Baby Blue Margaritas/Bobby's Last Kick
Various Beers/Assorted NUTS
Italian Stallion Crème Cake

A BABY BLUE POKER NIGHT

ALCAPONI ANTIPASTA
Arrange all the following on a colorful platter
Shape
for a delicious and filling appetizer:
Thin slices of salami   Cherry tomatoes
Ripe Olives   Radishes   Artichokes
Celery hearts   Anchovy   Deviled eggs
Assorted cheeses Thin slices of roast beef
And any other tidbit, like scallions.

POKER SALAD
Chop all the following ingredients as you desire,
Place in a salad bowl, cover and refrigerate:
2 ripe tomatoes   1 green pepper   2 scallions
1 can artichoke hearts, drained   1 cucumber
4 strips of crispy cooked bacon season with
Black pepper and a seasoning supreme.

When ready to serve:
Wash and tear 1 bunch red and green
leafy lettuce into bite size pieces.
Add to above. Sprinkle with
Parmesan/Romano cheese. Add
your favorite Italian Dressin'.
PW

ITALIAN MEATBALLS
Combine all the following. Mix well.

into balls. Bake for 20 to 25 min. at 350.
PLOP into a bowl of hot Marinara Sauce!
1 lb. Lean ground beef or turkey
$\frac{1}{4}$ cup seasoned breadcrumbs
$\frac{1}{2}$ tsp. chopped basil
Dash of pepper/salt
1 clove crushed garlic
$\frac{1}{4}$ cup Parmesan cheese

MARINARA SAUCE
Cook the following in hot oil until tender:
1 large chopped onion
2 finely chopped carrots
2 cloves minced garlic

Add the following. Bring to a boil.
Simmer, uncover for 45 to 60 minutes.
2 28-oz. cans tomatoes.....diced
1 tsp. Oregano/Red Pepper/Black Pepper
HAVE THAT CRUSTY BREAD READY FOR
SOPPIN' UP THE SAUCE!!

13

HARDROLLER EGGPLANT LASAGNA

You already gotcha sauce for this particular Lasagna…Marinara. So begin by boiling 1 package lasagna noodles in salted water until done. Drain. Meanwhile, slice a large eggplant, with skin intact, into thin rounds….do the same with a medium onion. Saute in olive oil until almost tender. While thats doing, add 1 pt. Ricotta or Cottage Cheese to 1 beaten egg. Now you are ready to make your Lasagna:

Layer noodles in a lightly greased, 3 qt. rectangular casserole. Spread a portion of the cheese/egg mixture, then some of the sauteed eggplant and onion, and some of your marinara. REPEAT until its all used up. Top with lots of your favorite yellow cheese slices and 'molto' Parmesan Cheese. BENISSIMO! Great!

ITALIAN STALLION CRÈME CAKE

You got to have the following: 1 cup Buttermilk   1 tsp. Baking Soda   1 stick Butter   ½ cup Shortening
2 cups Granulated Sugar or equal amount of Splenda   5 Eggs   2 cups sifted Flour   1 tsp. Vanilla
1 cup chopped Pecans   1 small can Coconut
And you will need the following for this luscious icing:
8 Oz. Pkg. Cream Cheese   1 stick butter   1 lb. Box Powdered Sugar   1 tsp. Vanilla

Mix the milk and soda…set aside. Cream the sugar, butter, and shortening. Add eggs and beat well. Add milk and flour a little at a time. Beat the vanilla, nuts, and coconut into the mixture. Pour the batter into 3 well-greased round baking pans and bake this yummy cake at 325 ° for approximately 25 minutes. You should know your oven if you've been cookin' for your Bob, so be careful and don't over do it!

Cool and Ice your moist Italiano cake by:
Creaming the butter and cream cheese until smooth and fluffy, then adding the Powdered sugar and Vanilla.
Beat well. YOU ARE READY TO ENJOY!!!   PW

A LOUSEY COOKOUT

"Bob, you better turn your chicken over in that marinade," yelled Susan from the shower. "They'll be here in a coupla hours." "Yeah, I will, but first I want you to try something new since you're already bathing, said Bob loudly over the falling water. "A new client, a soap salesman whos needin' a divorce, left me with all these 'great new product' samples…..he thought we'd love 'em." SlyTricksterBob had waited for the perfect opportunity…a steamy bathroom, a rushed schedule, a mind occupied with guests…yes, perfect to pull his dirty little trick!.

Susan didn't have time to disagree, reached out, grabbed this 'great new product, and began to lather up. Her head and body began to tingle and slightly sting. She thought the fragrance a bit strong on the chemicals, but Susan had her mind more on the guest coming for one of their famous Bob-O-ques. The backyard party was always surprising and rather tasty cause you never knew Who would leave with Whom!!!!! Food was pretty good too!

After showering Susan kept noticing that strange chemical smell about herself, but she had way too much to do to worry about it. Maybe the cleaners had used too much solution in that cute little sundress, and outside….. who would notice anyway! Little did Susan know that smell would follow her through all her chores and even mask the wonderful aroma of Bad Bob's Sassy Spicy Chicken.

Soon their guests were greeted with smiles and cheers, and words about Bob's great cookin' skills. He was good alright but it usually wasn't with food! All the party-goers kept commenting on the strong chemical smell…."Bob, did you just fertilize the lawn?"….."Remind me not to get that brand of charcoal lighter!"….."New perfume Susan?" Susan began to feel somewhat self-conscious and concerned. She would find a moment to check herself…curiosity and 'the smell' were about to get to her!

When everyone was full with food and drink Susan slipped to her bathroom to better examine this 'great new product.' She searched for her bifocals which seemed to be hidden from sight. They were no where to be found and she could hardly see to read without them. Could this have been what Rooster Man was countin' on???? She remembered her magnifying glass in the sewing basket and proceeded to read the small print on the 'new, revolutionary body soap, guaranteed to RID YOUR BODY OF LICE', better known as CRABS in the illicit world of cheaters or Entomologists. Horrified, Susan jumped back into the shower and gave her occupied body another dose of this "great new product." The deceiving JackAss had gotten himself some new baggage of the creepy, crawly kind and brought em home to mama!!!!!

Well, the wet-headed, blonde Susan joined her guest smiling as though nothing had happened…she had plans for the

GREAT CHEF AND HIS NEW BEST BUDDIES !!!!! Susan didn't dare go too close to the grill for fear of igniting, but she did manage to get very close to some of the Hot, Sexy Bods to see if they were using this same new shampoo. Had Bob picked up these new friends from one of my friends?????

TIP: Do Not Sleep With A Cheatin' JackAss Husband or any kinda partner!!!

RECIPES FOR:

German Pilsner Beers   Pitchers of Scotch Stingers   Buckets of Licey Icey Fruity Waters
          Smelly Susans Hot Crawley Crab Dip   Bite-Sized Asparagus Quiche

          SassySpicy BadBobs Canned Chicken   TricksterDickster Coleslaw
     Hot 'n Sexy Baked Beans   Rooster Mans Foil Wrapped Corn-the-Cob
          Bring Em Home To Mama Marinated Cucumber/Tomatoes/Onions
                    New Loaded Creepy Friends Potatoes

          Grasshopper Pie   Stingy Tingly Key Lime Tarts   PW

A LOUSEY COOKOUT

WHOOPS!!!
1 pt. cream
½ lb. grated Swiss cheese
1 T. Sherry

SMELLY SUSAN'S HOT CRAWLY CRAB DIP

Melt ya 1 stick of Butter and saute 1 small bunch of Green Onions with ½ cup chopped, fresh parsley. Add 2 T Flour and rest of ingredients. Stir in the Crabmeat. Serve in a chafing dish to keep it warm. GREAT with those lil chicken biscuit crackers!

TRICKSTERDICKSTER COLESLAW

Mix together the following for a great little Slaw:
1 lg. Bag finely chopped Cabbage   3 to 5 T Vinegar
1 ½ t Salt   ½ t Mustard   pinch or more Sugar
2 T Sour Cream   2 T Mayonnaise Give a GOOD Chilling
      Kinda like Good Ol BOB does to ya!!!

SASSYSPICY BADBOBS CANNED CHICKEN

Getcha how ever many whole chickens you need. Getcha the same amount of your favorite beers and drink about 1/3 of each . Sit ya a little chicken on top of each 2/3 full beer. Baste each chickadee with your Favorite Bob-O-Que sauce or just Canola oil with salt, pepper, garlic, or any other seasoning you favor. Sit 'em on the grill, can UP of course and just watch 'em turn into a scrumptious DELIGHT! KEEP 'EM OFF DIRECT FLAMES.

BITE-SIZED ASPARAGUS QUICHE

Prick a few holes in about a doz. Pastry tarts. Bake at 375° until slightly brown. When done place canned, drained and patted Asparagus Tips in the bottom of each lil cup Meantime, beat 2 lg. Eggs and 2 lg. Egg yolks with 1 ¼ cups of half-and-half. Add a pinch of: salt, pepper, nutmeg and 1 cup Swiss cheese. THERE IT IS! Pour into those little Jokers and bake until the custard is puffed, golden and set. YUM!

HOT 'n SEXY BAKED BEANS

To 2 Lg. Cans of baked beans in tomato sauce, add 1 lb. Cooked, drained sausage, ¼ cup brown sugar, 2 t salt, 1 t dry mustard and 1 t yellow prepared mustard. Also throw in about ¼ cup molasses or corn syrup Its no telling which one you've got after foolin' with a BOB!

Dont forget to dump in ½ cup onion and ½ cups Catsup. Cook at 350 for about an hour...covered. For a crusty top, kinda like ol BOB, uncover about the last 15 minutes.
OUT OF SIGHT DELICIOUS!!!

PW

NEW LOADED CREEPY FRIENDS POTATOES

Purchase a large tub of already prepared mashed potatoes.

Mix together and lightly heat: 3 oz cream cheese   ¼ C milk   14 oz can chopped, drained Artichokes

¼ C mayonnaise   1/3 C chopped onions   2 t minced garlic   ¼ C parmesan cheese   1 lb. Crab meat

Mix with mashed potatoes and scoop mixture into individual baking dishes or 1 nice casserole dish.

Top with a pat of butter and a good shake of parmesan cheese or your favorite shredded yellow and heat on 400°
for about 20 minutes or until golden.

BRING 'EM HOME TO MAMA MARINATED CUCUMBER/TOMATOES/ONIONS

Wash and Cut: Cucumbers into rounds/ Tomatoes in wedges/ Purple Onion into thin slices. Place in a clear bowl and
marinate in your favorite Italian dressin' or a mixture of Olive n Vinegar. CHILL! CHILL! CHILL! SO PRETTY!

ROOSTER MANS FOIL WRAPPED CORN-ON-THE-COB

You will be loosely wrapping 8 to 10 ears of husked corn with individual pieces of aluminum foil . Before sealing:
generously coat with lots of butter and a sprinkling of seasoned salt. Place on the grill and give em about
30 min.....turn occasionaly to cook evenly. YUMMY, YUMMY BUTTERY GOOD!!!

GRASSHOPPER PIE

Over low heat cook together: 6 ½ C teeny marshmallows and ¼ C milk until marshmallows are melted. Cool and stir
every 5 minutes. Combine ¼ C crème de menthe liqueur and 2 T crème de cacao into the marshmallow mixture. Fold
In 2 C of whipped crème. Mix well...you'll probably want to eat it NOW, but instead pour it into a chilled prepared
Chocolate crust. Just like a grasshopper it'll be jumpin' outa that pan!!!

STINGY TINGLY KEY LIME TARTS

Lets make it easy on ourselves like all Bob's do....Mix up a good Key Lime Puddin' as the directions allow and dump it
into mini baked pastry tarts. Cover with a flavored whipped crème. CHILL EM, CHILL OUT, SERVE! They'll LOVE 'EM!

                                                                                    PW

A SHORT RIDE

"Bob, I dont know where your keys are," Nancy sternly said to her loose-goose husband, all the while laughing inside. She was determined to keep the travelin' soul home this beautiful spring night. Jack and Ginger needed another parent sometimes, even if it was their wandering father. So, Nancy had hidden all the keys to all the vehicles, or so she thought! This would force Daddy BobO to play with the kids or pretend to anyway. At least they would get to see him!

As Nancy prepared the quick and easy backyard dinner she could hear the motor of the mower moving swiftly through the neighbors yard. She couldn't wait to smell the freshly cut grass mingled with the aroma of great burgers on the grill. Arms full of yummies, Nancy made her way through the basement into the park like atmosphere of the backyard. She took a deep breath but there was no fresh scent of mowed grass, only the odor of exhaust. Strange! Nancy looked around hoping to find Bob and the kids engrossed in play, but there was Jack and Gin climbing the tree house, and NO BOB!

"Where's Daddy?" she yelled. In unison they said, "He's trying out the golf cart…he'll be right back." Dang it! I had forgotten about that overused cart…it never crossed my blonde mind! But the forces in the Universe were at play! Headin' straight for the Moose Club, PuttPutt Bob got only two miles down the road when the police forced him over. What a laugh they must have had! Before headin' out, the Sly Fox had grabbed my fuzzy white hat with pom pom ties and plopped it on his head thinking he needed a helmet!!!

After giving him a ticket for obvious reasons, they turned BoBob the Clown around and escorted him home, sirens blastin'! My two little children had their treat for the night. And Bob, red-faced and always red-eyed, spent the night playing with those innocent angels, and even got to eat dinner with 'em…another great surprise that was even better than the siren with blue flashin' lights.

TIPS: Sometimes getting caught is a good thing, particularly when it's a Bobcatchin'.

RECIPES FOR:

PW

Daddy BobO Burgers	BoBob Clown Slaw	PomPom Taters	Fuzzy White Coconut Cake 'n Blue Ice Cream
	Favorite Trimmin's	Nancys Surprise Baked Beans	Travelin' Bob Onion Dip 'n Chips
		Fresh Squeezed Lemonade	

A SHORT RIDE

DADDY BOBO BURGERS

Blend the following ingredients well and form into
12 large burgers: 3 lbs lean ground round   4 eggs
    2 small chopped onions   2 cloves minced garlic
    2 T Chili sauce   2 T your choice Mustard
    2 T Worcestershire or Steak sauce and Seasoned Salt
Cook burgers on greased grill to your liking...of course
BOB likes it near RAW since he's such an animal!!!

BOBOB CLOWN SLAW

Mix ALL together for a luscious dish:
    12 oz. Pkg. Broccoli Slaw   1 C seedless Red grapes
    1 chopped apple   2 peeled/sectioned Mandarin oranges
    ½ C toasted pecans   1 C Poppy Seed dressing CHILL IT!

POMPOM TATERS

Heat 2 T butter, 1 T garlic, 1 T Rosemary, 1 tsp Thyme in a
Dutch oven or skillet. Add 2 lbs partially peeled new potatoes.
Toss all together then place in a 425° oven for 30 minutes...
covered. Stir occasionally like BOB stirs-up your life. Add
your favorite Balsamic Vinaigrette, salt and pepper. Uncover
and roast for about 10 more minutes. LOVE IT!

PW

Trim those delicious burgers with:
    Cheese, Pickles, Tomato slices,
    Olives, Onion, Lettuce, Catsup,
    Mustard, Mayonnaise and whatever
    else you like...could be most anything!
Serve it all on a big, fat, sesame seed, whole
    grain' bun, BETTER FOR YA!

NANCY'S SURPRISE BAKED BEANS

Mix following and bake at 350° for 45 minutes: 1 chopped Onion   ½ lb cooked bacon   2 28oz cans bold 'n spicy Baked beans   1 15oz can drained black beans 1 15oz can drained kidney beans   3 C prepared BBQ sauce   ½ C firmly packed brown sugar   ¼ C mustard 1 t black/red pepper   2 t powdered garlic/parsley

TRAVELIN' BOB ONION DIP 'N CHIPS

Stir all the following together...Chill...and you have a goody! Small container Sour Cream   2 thin-sliced scallions 2 T chopped cilantro   1 tsp lime juice and 1 tsp grated rind Salt/pepper to taste.   Purple Chips are COOL!!!

FUZZY WHITE COCONUT CAKE

Mix 1 white cake mix as recipes calls. Bake in rectangular pan. After baking poke holes all over the warm cake. Pour 1 can Condensed milk all over the top, making sure it sinks into the holes. Meanwhile whip 8 oz cream cheese with 1 lg container whipped cream. Spread mixture over almost cooled cake. Top with lots of moist, canned coconut.
WHAT A CAKE FOR ANYTIME!

PW

BLUE ICE CREAM

Buy your favorite Vanilla ice cream. Allow it to get very soft. Mash 1 C blended fresh blueberries into the cream. Stir and twirl and refreeze for a cool, cool treat.

FRESH SQUEEZED LEMONADE

Boil 1 ½ C sugar and 2 ½ fresh lemon juice with 2 C water until sugar is dissolved. Add 8 more cups of water and cool. Before serving, add ice, lemon slivers, and fresh mint.
EVEN BOB WILL LOVE IT JUST PLAIN AND COLD!!!

ACCIDENTLY ON PURPOSE

Bob would SLAM BANG through the kitchen looking like Death-Eating-A-Teacake.....his voice would be low and Evil. You could feel the temperature drop drastically as icicles formed on the light fixtures. Horns would start growing from his head as he yelled, "I'm outta here!" Scary, NO.....Crazy, YES!!!

BeelzeBob thought he had bamboozled me! Actually, I had caught on to this Dog and Pony Act long ago......it was Rendevous Time for Chickie and Dickie, a match Made-in-Hell! For a split second that day, I thought about following him to his 'Minor-league Passion Pit,' but I'd already seen everything there was to see about Cockamamie Butthead Bob! He had tried to pull 'the wool over my eyes' too many times.....frankly, I just didn't give-a-flip anymore.

Jack and Ginger asked a few questions about Daddy and I told them he was out WORKIN' HARD, which was an understatement if there ever was one! We just fired up the grill, heated the stove, and went to cookin'. Delicious mussels, shrimp, crab, and pastas with fantastic sauces were practically jumpin' out of the pan! Neighbors, friends, and relatives came to partake of the glorious Feast. BOB WOULD HAVE LOVED IT! TOO BAD!!!

TIP: Even a Blind Hog catches an acorn every once in awhile!

RECIPES FOR:

  MuscleHead Mussel Chowder   Passion Pasta with Spicy Shrimp   Slam-Bam-Thank-You-Maam Clams
         Cockamamie Crab Cakes   Kiss-My-Grits Shrimp   Jerk Jam

LC

ACCIDENTLY ON PURPOSE

MUSCLE-HEAD MUSSEL CHOWDER

1 can of mussels   1 fish bouillon   2 minced garlic cloves   4 chopped green onions with tops 1 C of White Wine 3 C of chicken broth   ¼ C of heavy cream   2 T of butter   1 C chopped mushrooms   2 T flour 2 chopped tomatoes   4 chopped green onions withy tops   1 pack of dill seasoning. Melt butter in pan....stir in flour and make roux.   Add wine, broth, and heavy cream.....FLIP IN ALL THE OTHER INGREDIENTS EXCEPT THE MUSSELS. Bring to a boil.....reduce heat and simmer 4-5 minutes to consistency of chowder. ADD MUSSELS , SERVE THE LITTLE DARLINGS TO SOMEONE WHO LOVES YOU !

COOCKAMAMIE CRAB CAKES

1 to 1 ½ lbs. of crab-picked and drained   ¾ C mayo   ¾ C breadcrumbs   3 green onions chopped fine   1 egg beaten   dash of cayenne pepper   ½ T chopped parsley   1 t spicy mustard   1 t lemon juice   Combine all ingredients.....Shape into patties.....fry in hot oil until gloriously golden brown. Drain on paper towel and serve. CRAZY, WANNABE SCARY BOB loved my crab cakes. Maybe, CHICKIE, whipped him up some...crab cakes too !

PASSION PASTA WITH SPICY SHRIMP

2 T olive oil   2 minced garlic cloves   ¼ C parsley   4 chopped green onions with tops   ¼ t cayenne pepper   ½ of each, red, yellow, green bell pepper, seeded and chopped   ½ C White Wine   2 T lemon juice   2t Worcestershire sauce   1 stalk chopped celery   1 lb. medium to large shrimp ...peeled and deveined. Saute garlic , celery, bell pepper and onion in olive oil, 3-4 minutes. Add wine, lemon juice , cayenne pepper, Worcestershire sauce ... stirring as needed....3-4 minutes. Add shrimp and cover... cook over low heat till it turns pink... 3-5 minutes. Serve over angle hair pasta... chopped parsley garnish. This dish would knock BOB THE BUTTEHEAD out....he always wanted more....but isn't that just the way it is, you can't have your pasta and your bimbo too. Of course, BOBOs bimbo was as common as pig tracks and didnt know a shrimp from an alligator. I coulda told her which one OLD BOBBY BOY liketa think he was. He always reminded me of THE BIG BAD WOLF, THE ONE WITH THE BIG OLD TEETH!

LC

SLAM-BAM-THANK-YOU-MA'AM-CLAMS

2 LBS. cleaned clams   3T butter   3T oil   1 medium chopped onion   2 cloves of minced garlic   dash of garlic powder   2C White Wine or 12 oz. beer. Sweat onions and garlic in oil and butter over low heat….4-5 minutes. Add wine or beer. Add clams. Cook covered until clam shell pops open…serve with crusty bread. FOOL AROUND BOB MISSED THE PARTY ONE MORE TIME !

KISS MY GRITS SHRIMP

1 C uncooked quick cookin' grits $\frac{1}{4}$ C butter   3C of water   1 lb. medium shrimp…peeled and deveined   1 clove minced garlic $\frac{1}{2}$ t salt $\frac{1}{2}$ t white pepper   2t paprika   2T olive oil   juice of 1 lemon. Coat shrimp in mixture of garlic, salt, pepper and paprika. Heat olive oil …. toss shrimp in pan ….cooking until shrimp turns pink. Fix grits according to package directions….add butter and stir. Serve in bowls….grits topped with shrimp…lemon juice squeezed on shrimp. YAW-LL R FIXIN' TA EAT SOUTHERN STYLE !

JERK JAMBALAYA

1lb. sausage links cut in quarters   1 can chicken broth   1 16oz. can crushed tomatoes with juice   1 C water $\frac{1}{4}$ t hot pepper sauce $\frac{1}{2}$ green pepper cut in strips $\frac{1}{2}$ C chopped onion   1 clove minced garlic $\frac{1}{4}$ t each; thyme, allspice, cloves, cayenne pepper.   1 lb. medium shrimp… peeled and deveined 2 chicken breast …cooked … cut in pieces. Using a large skillet, brown sausage, pour off fat. Add all ingredients EXCEPT shrimp, chicken, bell pepper. Bring to a boil-cover …. Cook… 10 minutes. Add shrimp, green pepper and chicken…cook 10 minutes more or till rice is done. Stir occasionally while cooking. I have been known to cheat, using instant rice at the last minute… worked fine for me. JERKY WAS ALL FIRED UP MOST OF THE TIME…HE WOULDN,T KNOW IF I HAD USED RICE OR RAISINS!

LC

24

BLACK LACE AND PROMISES

Twice a month I would travel with Jack and Gin to the Big City where the Doctors actually knew your head from your tail! My parents were always willing to help with these appointments and would beg us to spend the night. Of course we would... I loved and missed them so, and they were my allies! Years ago they pleaded with me to leave Narcissistic Bob. In fact, they NEVER wanted me to marry him in the first place! I remember that fateful Valentines Day I wore my engagement ring into our home. Mother and Daddy both, tearfully left the room. I can still hear Janie, my sister-in-law, ask, "Where's the diamond?". The most intolerable act toward the whole family, they would argue, was when, "The boy would come into the den where we were all watchin TV, and invariably turn the channel without so much as a word....dat blame him!!!".

Before leaving my hometown, my dear old parents would pack a great home cooked dinner, knowing we would arrive late, and positively being certain that the Boy would not be home, much less have any food waiting! "Ol Bob sure hadn't got any talent for Home cookin' or anything else HOME....Sissy, why did you marry that Boy?", Daddy would often say, shaking his head. And no, there was NEVER food ready when we arrived, but there was always a SURPRISE!

I might be blonde, but every single time I'd come home from those overnight outings, the contents of my pretty, smelly-good, underwear drawer would be ransacked, and one or two of my Lovelies would be missing! "You're losing it!", Bob would always say. "I havent even been here!" Well, that was true, when we were home anyway! If pets could only talk!!!!

Women know these things, I mean about their underwear! We fantasize wearing those dainty, lacey black, or sexy red velvet pieces and being the object of our husband's affection. My imagination was about all I had! All my pretties invariably stayed in the drawer, in the same position. THEY NEVER MOVED, that is until I went out-of-town!!! They were just waitin' for that hopeful, special day when the occasion might ARISE!

Well, IT did ARISE....every time I left town! Bob either turned to Bobette when we left overnight and was wearing my sexy undies beneath his business pinstripes....or BadBob had a playmate who liked my STUFF better than hers, theirs, them, whatever! It wasn't OK, but my caring had just about gone by the wayside, just like my pretty undies! No more questioning, no more fantasizing about BobbyBoy anyway, just wondering every time I saw a pretty young client or a flirty neighbor or friend..."Is she wearing my bra and panties?".

The next time I planned an appointment in the Big City I also planned a Big Surprise for my OLD underwear drawer and its contents. I found a big patch of poison ivy and rubbed every last pretty in the juice of the irritant. I also rubbed the inside of the drawer before placing the black and red sexy pieces back as neatly as ever. I couldn't wait to see who would be itchin' the most, Bobette or the PlaymateThief!!!

TIP: If you're allergic to The Ivy, you could place a few of those eatable panties and a cheap cupless bra in your drawer
 next time you're leavin' town...give em a thrill!!! Or you could stick a few thorns in the right places!!!
 Always keep BIG cans of disinfectant on hand...in the bedroom, and keep clean, sanitized sheets hidden and waitin'.
 Better yet, STOP SLEEPING WITH THE JACKASS!!!!

RECIPES FOR:

Fantasy Pork Chops   In-Your-Pants Potatoes

Payback Peas   Mamatas Fritatas   Early Rising Rolls

Narcissistic Noodles   Dat Blame Good Sweet Tea

Sexy Red Velvet Cake   Black Lace Cookies with Plunderin' Pudding

PW

BLACK LACE AND PROMISES

FANTASY PORK CHOPS

For a GREAT tasting chop, combine ¼ C all purpose flour with 1 t seasoned salt and ¾ t seasoned pepper. Flop 'n coat 4 thick boneless pork chops in this mixture. Cook 'em in olive oil until each side is a golden brown. Move 'em out and add 3 or 4 minced garlic to the oil...saute for just a minute. Add 1/3 C balsamic vinegar and 1/3 C chicken broth to the garlic. Stir around the goodies on the bottom of the skillet then add 3 diced plum tomatoes and 2 T capers. Dump the pork chops back into the skillet. Reduce the heat...cover...simmer until pork is done...5 to 10 minutes.

IN-YOUR-PANTS-POTATOES

Scrub and Cut 4 Yukon Potatoes into ¼ inch rounds. Place the rounds in a single layer in a rectangular, greased baking pan. Mix ¼ C melted butter, 2 T grated onion, 1 t salt and pepper together and pour over the potatoes. Cover with Foil and bake at 400° for 25 to 30 minutes. TEST BY POKING WITH A FORK LIKE YOU WOULD WITH BOB!

PAYBACK PEAS

Mix ALL the following together then dump into a greased casserole ...top with bread crumbs and dot with butter. Bake at 350° for about 30 minutes.

1 chopped onion   ½ green pepper   1 stick butter
4 chopped celery stalks   1 4oz can mushroom pieces
1 lg can cream of mushroom soup
1 2oz jar pimentos...chopped/drained
2 17oz cans drained English peas

MAMATAS FRITATAS

Mix all the following together then dump into a well-buttered quiche dish or lg pie pan and bake at 350° for about 35 minutes:

2 cubed zucchini   2 cubed yellow squash
1 medium chopped onion   1 t salt/pepper
12 beaten eggs   ½ C sour cream
1/3 C chopped fresh basil
WARM OR COLD.....FANTASTIC!

EARLY RISING ROLLS

Place 1 pkg yeast in 2 C warm water, NOT HOT. Add 1 beaten egg, ¼ C sugar, 1 ½ sticks butter, 4 C self-risin' flour. Mix well then drop into greased muffin pan and bake the lil' sweeties for 25 minutes.   LOVE 'UM!

PW

NARCISSISTIC NOODLES

Cook ¾ lb thin spaghetti, drain and set aside. Over a low
Heat, combine the following: 6 T butter 3 T olive oil
  6 T minced parsley 6 T minced garlic (5 cloves)
  3 T basil ¼ t salt/black pepper 2 dashes cayenne
Add the cooked spaghetti and 1 ½ C parmesan cheese. Toss
to coat all the noodles. THIS WILL SUIT BOB JUST FINE!

SEXY RED VELVET CAKE

Mix everything below until there are NO lumps unlike BOB'S
head after he pulls a trick: 1 ½ C sugar 2 C canola oil
  2 beaten eggs 1 t vinegar 1 C buttermilk 2 t vanilla
  1 small bottle red food coloring 2 ½ C sifted flour
  1 t soda 1 t salt 2 T cocoa
Cook in 2 round pans at 350° for about 30 to 35 minutes.
Meantime...mix up the frosting for a cool cake icing:
  1 ½ sticks butter 1 8 oz cream cheese 1 T vanilla
  1 ½ boxes powdered sugar 1 C chopped pecans
BEST KEPT COOL LIKE YOU SHOULD BE WITH BOB!

BLACK LACE COOKIES

Combine 1 C butter, 1 ½ t vanilla, and ½ t salt
and blend. Beat 1 C sugar to mixture, then add
2 C all-purpose flour, 1 6 oz pkg semi-sweet
chocolate morsels, and ¼ C finely chopped pecan.
Mix well then press evenly onto an ungreased,
rectangular pan. Press about ¼ C coarser pecans
into the top. Bake at 375° for about 25 minutes.
COOL AND BREAK INTO IRREGULAR PIECES.
YUMMY! And goes great with some
creamy vanilla or butterscotch store-bought
PLUNDERIN' PUDDING

DAT BLAME GOOD SWEET TEA

Steep 6 small tea bags in boiling water...chunk the tea bags and add the following:
  1 ½ C sugar 1 6 oz can frozen orange juice 1 6 oz can frozen lemonade 1 6 oz pineapple juice
  10 C cold water Serve over lots of crushed ice.
  SO VERY REFRESHING AFTER SPENDING AN EXHAUSTIN' DAY WITH A BOB!!!

PW

THE BALL GAME #1

BouncingBalls Bob called from work to say he and some clients had tickets to the Big Ballgame and he'd probably be home no later than 10:00. "Don't wait up for me," he hurriedly said. I knew that ten o'clock usually meant anywhere from 12:00 AM 'til early daylight, so when the clock struck ten, Blondie Girl went to bed with a good book. Morning came...but not Bob! His side of the bed had not been touched. What better to make a perfectly good morning GO UGLY.....again!!!

As I drank my delicious, hot coffee, ate my fluffy omelet, and buttered my warm, healthy muffin, I could hear the car slowly pull into the drive. The door opened and sheepishly, there was ThreeStrikesYourOut Bob, baseball cap in-hand, and saying, "I couldn't make it home by 10:00 last night cause the game went into extra innings." I kept eating and reading as much BULL in the morning newspaper as RunForYourLife Bob was stuttering out!

TIP: Next time find someone to eat that fluffy omelet with you after having you own Home Game!
      Have your own Game Plan ready whenever a Baseball Bob pulls a stunt like this......like a baseball bat
      waitin' behind the door! A rolled-up newspaper will do just fine too!

RECIPES FOR:

RunForYourLife Bob Coffees:
Mexicano Bob Café   Viennese Bob Café   Bob's Au Lait Café Mix

Blondie Girls Special Home Game Omelets:
Puffy Fluffy Cheese/HERB Omelet   ThreeStrikes Peppers/Ham/Cheese Omelet

Early Early Morning Rise 'n Shine Muffins:
DoofusDandy BobMuffins   Extra Inning/Extra Whammy Muffins

PW

29

THE BALL GAME #1

RUNFOR YOUR LIFE BOB COFFEE:

BOB'S CAFÉ AU LAIT MIX
1/3 C instant coffee
½ C nondairy powdered coffee creamer
½ C sugar or splenda

CAFÉ VIENNESE
1 T BOB Au Lait Mix
1 T Cognac
A dash of nutmeg

CAFÉ MEXICANO
1 T BOB Au Lait Mix
1 T Kahlua
Dash of ground cinnamon
1 t grated semisweet chocolate

BLONDIE GIRLS SPECIAL HOME GAME OMELETS

PUFFY FLUFFY CHEESE/HERB OMELET
Beat 4 eggs. Add 2 T water, ¼ t salt,
1 T butter, 1/3 C milk, 1 t chives,
1 t Italian herb seasoning, ½ C Swiss
Cheese, ¼ C sour cream, 2 T white wine.
Beat well and pour into a buttered 10
inch skillet. Cook over low heat until puffy
and set. Fold one side over the other. Serve.
BE PROUD IF YOU CAN DO THIS!

THREE STRIKES PEPPERS/HAM/CHEESE OMELET
Beat 4 eggs and add 2 T water, ¼ salt,
1 T butter, 1/3 C milk. Add the following:
½ C diced cooked ham   1 3 oz can sliced mushrooms
1 3 oz cream cheese, 1 ½ t lemon juice, diced peppers
dash seasoned salt/pepper   1 t mustard
Cook exactly like PUFFY FLUFFY except:
Right before the eggs set, sprinkle entire mixture
with your favorite, shredded yellow cheese. Fold.

EARLY EARLY MORNING RISE 'N SHINE MUFFINS

DOOFUSDANDY BOBMUFFINS
Mix up this BOB-poppin' goody by combining:
2 ¼ C oat bran   1 t cinnamon   1 T baking powder
¼ C skim milk   ¼ C your favorite whiskey   2 T canola oil
2 eggs   ¾ C apple juice   ¼ C applesauce   ¼ C corn syrup
½ C chopped pecans   ½ C raisins Bake at 400° for about
20 minutes in a well-oiled muffin tin.....1 dozen.

EXTRA INNING/EXTRA WHAMMY MUFFINS
Mix well together: 2 C hammered all-bran cereal
1 ¾ C milk 1 ½ C all-purpose flour   ¾ C sugar
1 T baking powder   ¼ t salt   1 mashed ripe banana
½ C peanut butter   ½ C chopped pecans   1 lg egg
¼ C canola oil   Bake at 350° for 25 to 30 minutes
in a well-oiled muffin tin.....1 dozen.

PW

THE BALL GAME #2

Bob and Ruthie were newlyweds even though she was doubting the Sanctified Bond. Her so-called husband was NEVER home...work, play, trips, whatever, occupied his time. What happened to the thing called Wedding Bliss??? It was almost like Empty Nest Syndrome instead! And they didn't even have kids!!!

Bob called from the office to say he and some co-workers would be, "traveling to the Big Ballgame tonight and don't wait up cause the game is goin' into extra innings." He hung up quickly knowing Blonde Ruthie's knowledge of sports was very limited. "She would never catch that ball," Strikeout Bob thought to himself!

Near suppertime Ruthie's brother stopped by, as he sometimes did ,to hopefully be invited to dinner. Well, this sports illiterate Blonde had the night off from cookin' due to that Big Ballgame her brother Sam had just turned to on the TV. She fixed him a delicious leftover meatloaf sandwich and watched this supposed Great Game with him. Ruthie found herself actually enjoying it, but was surprised when the game ended with a whopping score of 8 to 2. Puzzled she asked Sam, "I thought the game was goin into extra innings?" He loudly gulped, spraying his beer all over himself as he asked, "What do you mean by that, Ruthie...I know the roots of your hair are NOT BLONDE!!!"

She explained her conversation with Bob earlier in the day. That night, Ruthie got sports educated! She also had a Great Game Plan waitin for Baseball Bob, WHENEVER he might be roundin' that corner for Home!!! He'd sure be regrettin' that Homerun Stretch for a long time!!!

TIPS: Get educated quick on anything and everything you JUST THINK your Bob is interested in! Hit yourself in the head with a BB Bat next time you believe ANYTHING a Bob says!!!

RECIPES FOR:

      Simpleton Meatloaf   Extra Inning Leftover Simpleton Meatloaf Sandwich

    Three Strikes Out Cheese Pasta Bake   Homerun Stretch Ice Cream Crepes

PW

THE BALL GAME # 2

EXTRA INNING LEFTOVER SIMPLETON MEATLOAF SANDWICH

Well, to have a leftover meatloaf sandwich you gotta start out with a Meatloaf...yes, I know you have a BOB, but I mean a REAL MEATLOAF!!! So here goes...a simple meatloaf, like BOB, but better!

In a large bowl, combine the following:
   1 ½ lbs lean ground beef or turkey   ¾ C quick cookin' oat meal   1 or 2 eggs
   ¾ C milk   ¼ C chopped onion   salt/pepper to taste   ¼ C green pepper or yellow or red
 Shape it and place in a loaf pan.
 Mix 1/3 C catsup with 2 T brown sugar and 1 T yellow mustard. Pour this mixture over the loaf.
Bake at 350° for 1 hour.   Now you have something to make a meatloaf sandwich with!!!
Take bread slices and spread with mayonnaise and a sprinkle of fresh basil. Add cold meatloaf slices, lettuce and tomato.

THREE STRIKES OUT CHEESE PASTA BAKE

Prepare a 16 oz package Zita or Penne pasta as directions indicate. Drain and return to the pot.
Stir 2 10 oz bottles Alfredo sauce and 1 8 oz container sour cream with the pasta. Dump half the mixture into a greased rectangular baking dish. Mix together 1 15 oz container Ricotta cheese, 2 eggs, ¼ C Romano cheese, and ¼ C chopped basil.
Spread over the pasta mixture then spoon the remaining pasta mix over the cheese layer. Top with 1 ½ C Mozzarella Cheese. Bake at 350° for 30 minutes or so....you'll know when its bubbly. WONDERFULLY CHEESY LIKE BOB CAN BE!

HOMERUN STRETCH ICE CREAM CREPES

You need prepared Crepes for this WOW dessert. Microwave as many crepes as you need on HIGH for 10 seconds.
Warm 3 T hot fudge topping for each crepe. Dobble 1 C chocolate ice cream in the center of each crepe. Wrap crepe around the ice cream then place it seam down on a pretty dessert plate, that is for everyone EXCEPT FOR BOB. HIS GOES ON A FLIMSY PAPER PLATE THAT WILL GET SOGGY AND FALL IN HIS LAP!   HA! HA! HA!
Top those pretties with lines of hot fudge sauce and strawberries, raspberries, or blue berries OR ALL OF 'UM! ALL THE BETTER FOR STAINING HIS CLOTHES!   HE! HE! HE!

PW

A BLEACHED BLONDE ANNIVERSARY

"I can't believe this keeps on happenin' over and over again!", cried MaryLou. "I just can't take it anymore." MaryLou had just spent every dime she had on groceries for a candlelight dinner. You see, it was BrazenBob and MaryLou's Wedding Anniversary. "I walked outta that grocery store and damn, that Jackass passed right by me, and HE NEVER SAW ME!", exclaimed ML to her friend Louise! "He didn't see me cause some Hag from Hell was sittin' on top him in that fancy, new Red pickup truck of his!", she bawled! "He and that lil' Mama were laughing and kissin'....they almost had a wreck!"

MaryLou continued to make the scene as real to Louise as she could and her temper just flared more and more 'til she stated, "I'm gonna get even with that disgusting, low-life, cheating, no-good JackaBob....I'm gonna fix him good, AND that blessed dinner from Hell too," she screamed. "Just you wait Mr. Boob-Lovin", Strangelove Bobby!" As anyone could see, MaryLou had been humiliated enough, and ol' BobbyBoy was in Hot water just like that rice she was cooking. All the while she was fixin' her famous Creamy Island Chicken, MaryLou just kept planning and plotting.

You see, Bob was quite a hunter, not only of Big Boobed women, but Big-Horned Game. He could catch prize-winning fish with the best of the experts, or so HE claimed. After all, when he came back from those 'expeditions,' heads and tails filled his shiny new Red pickup truck. Funny though, they were always mounted and ready for hanging. That in itself drew ML's suspicion! But after all Bob, The Great White Hunter knew more about this stuff than she did. You know, MaryLou was just Bob's Dumb Blonde Wife!!!!

He would tell her, "This great taxidermist fellow travels with us and fixes these heads and fish right on the Spot!!!!". At this, ML's stare would be just as blank as the poor dead animals, not because she didn't know better, but just the thought that he thought she was swallowing such a tale!!! Their walls in the den were filled with fin, feathers, and racks. You could hardly walk by one of these stiffs, that it didn't mess up your hair or pull your ball cap right off. Brave Bob would just sit for hours admiring his prey! MaryLou would sit for moments and think about the walls caving in!!!!

Still fuming and fussin', MaryLou finished preparing the scrumptious dinner. LoverBoy finally made it home with NO flowers, NO gifts, NO NOTHING for the five years she had spent in Hell!! As the Silent Partners were finishing the special, no-candled dinner, Cheatin' Bob said, "I think I'm gonna plop myself in bed 'cause it's been a really tiring day". He never once said a word about their anniversary!

But, this Jackass putting himself to bed fit right into MaryLou's plan, just perfectly!!! When his deep snoring began, ML started her sinister work....and it wasn't to clean the kitchen! Ever so quietly she unloaded the den of Bob's prideful heads and tails and placed them into the bed of his shiny, new Red pickup. There were so many of them, she had to place some in the cab of the vehicle. With this plan in mind, MaryLou had earlier traveled back to the store and bought them out of Bleach. Red eyes gleaming and teeth clinched, she poured every speck of that color-outter over every stiff species in the cab and in the bed of that pretty, new shiny, Red pickup. It now looked as if Bob had been hookin' or shootin' every albino species in the county! The once mounted beasts were now all Blondies!!!! Bob would be reminded of MaryLou for a long time!

By this time, MaryLou was looking kinda pale herself, and her clothes looked like they had been bought at the local tie-dye store, but she just laughed at the sight. Proudly, she snuck back into the dark house, picked up her bags she'd packed before preparing The Last Supper, and headed to her shiny, new Pale-Yellow Sports Car. It would speed her away to some White Sandy Beach Paradise and Freedom!

TIP: Keep lots of Bleach on hand for who knows what!   Keep a little $stash$ around for quick get-a-ways!

RECIPES FOR:

MaryLou's Before Dinner Red Pick-Me-Ups   Ball-Bustin' Appetizer
White Creamy Island Chicken   Albino Butter Bean Bake
Wild Paradise White Rice   Sparkling White Champagne
Quick Pale Brownies with White Hard Sauce
Marinated Red Tomatoes/White Onions/Peeled Cucumbers

PW

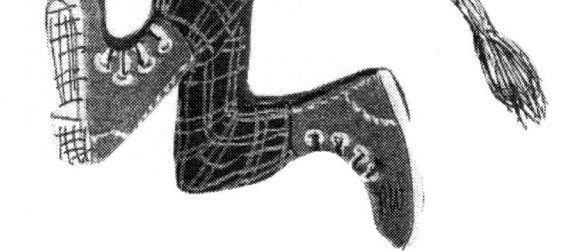

A BLEACHED BLONDE ANNIVERSARY

BALL-BUSTIN' APPETIZER
Sauté 2 thinly sliced lg onions with 4 minced garlic cloves until tender. Add 1 28 oz can diced tomatoes, ½ seeded, chopped jalapeno pepper, 1 t chopped chipotle peppers in adobo sauce, 2 t more adobo sauce, 1 drained can whole corn, ¼ C chopped cilantro, 2 T lime juice. Bring to a boil. Reduce heat and simmer, covered for 10 minutes. Stir…Stir…Stir. Chill overnight for better flavor. Serve with Blue Corn Chips.
GUARANTEED TO SET BOB ON FIRE!!!

WHITE CREAMY ISLAND CHICKEN
Layer 1 jar chipped beef slices in a rectangular Pyrex. Wrap 4 to 6 skinless chicken breasts with 1 piece of bacon each. Place chicken on top beef. Mix: 1 lg cream cheese   1 C Real mayonnaise   1 lg can cream of chicken soup ¼ C lemon juice or cooking sherry   1 C Parmesan cheese Heat mixture and blend well. Pour over chicken. Cover tightly with foil and bake at 325° for about 1 hour.   TO DIE FOR!!!

WILD PARADISE WHITE RICE
Cook 2 C of long grain white rice as directions indicate. When ready, pour the gravy from the Island Chicken all Over. One bite and you will think you have DIED AND GONE TO HEAVEN!

ALBINO BUTTER BEAN BAKE
Cook 2 10 oz pkg frozen butter or lima beans according to the directions. Drain when cooked and set aside. Cook ¼ C chopped onion, 3 T butter, 1 C herb-seasoned stuffing mix with 1/3 C water. Stir in 1 C sour cream, 1 T flour, 2/3 C milk, ½ C shredded Cheddar cheese. Mix EVERYTHING together…DON'T FORGET THE BEANS! Plop the mix into a greased casserole and top with a handful of cheese and sprinkles of some more stuffin' mix.
Bake uncovered at 350° for about 20 minutes. SURE IS GOOOOOOOOD!
PW

MARINATED RED TOMATOES/WHITE ONIONS/PEELED CUCUMBER

Peel 3 cucumbers and thinly slice.   Thinly slice 2 celery stalks.   Core 1 small green and 1 small red pepper, and thinly slice both.   Thinly slice 1 lg red onion and do the same with 1 large tomato.   Place all the slices in a large glass bowl and sprinkle with 1 ½ T salt.   Bring 1 C sugar, 1 C white vinegar, 1 t celery seed, and ½ t mustard seed to a boil , stirring constantly until the sugar dissolves. COOL about an hour, then pour over the vegetables.
        Cover and CHILL for at least 2 hours like you would if BOB GOT OUT OF IT!!!

QUICK PALE BROWNIES WITH WHITE HARD SAUCE

Heat: 1 lb light brown sugar with 4 eggs until sugar dissolves...DO NOT BOIL.
 Remove from heat and add: 2 C Bisquick   2 t vanilla   1 ½ C chopped pecans
Pour into a greased 9 x 13 pan and bake at 325° for 30 minutes. Cool. Cut and top with following sauce.

Cream 1 stick butter and gradually beat in 3 C sugar until creamy and sugar has dissolved.
Beat in a pinch of salt and the good part.....1/3 C your favorite Whiskey.

        DELICIOUS OVER POUND CAKE TOO OR JUST BY ITSELF OVER NOTHIN'.

                                                                                        PW

BEWARE OF EVIL EYE

RobotRobert was not known for his obliging attitude or kind heart. Therefore, it came as no surprise when we were on a family outing…and I use that term loosely…that Mr. Perfect was extremely annoyed with Crystal. It seems our youngest was complaining of a tummy-ache and the 'bellyaching' got under Bob's skin. My maternal instinct kicked in, full force, and I gave Non-compassionate Bob the Evil Eye. He finally decided that to prevent a catastrophe, he better Stop. Even with his limited, shallow-brained, asinine intellect, Bob knew when to Pull-Up!

Strangely, the very next morning Ol Bob began to have an uneasy feeling in his lower abdomen, somewhat similar to Crystal's queasiness the night before. Secretly, I had added a creamy, white, liquid laxative to his other wise dull bowl of cornflakes. Believe me, I told Bathroom Bob with great enthusiasm! He was downright speechless…..that was a first!

Crystal, Jack, and Ginger sat down to an incredible feast of breakfast delights. I fried country ham, fixed fancy French toast with strawberries and cream, scrambled eggs 'n cheese, whipped-up buttery grits, sausage, gravy, and fluffy hot biscuits. They were eatin' high-on-the-Hog while Bob was turning various shades of green.

Justice was served along with the Orange Juice!!!

TIP: Be nice and nice will come back to you…..be ugly and ugly will get you in the END!

RECIPES FOR:

    Tummy Pleasin' French Toast with Berries   Nitty Gritty Grits   Gotcha' Scrambled Eggs 'n Cheese
         Hothead Biscuits and Sausage Gravy   Hog Wild Country Ham

LC

BEWARE OF EVIL EYE   LC

TUMMY   PLEASIN'   FRENCH TOAST   WITH   BERRIES

6 slices French bread   3 eggs   ½ C half/half   1 C milk   ½ t cinnamon   1 banana   1 pint fresh strawberries 1 can whipped cream   1 T butter.   Combine   eggs...milk... half/half...cinnamon... banana in a food processor. Dip slices   of   bread   into   mixture. Melt   butter   in   skillet... brown   French bread... serve... top with whipped cream n strawberries.   BOB WAS POSITIVELY IN A STUPOR EYE BALLIN' THE FEAST

NITTY GRITTY GRITS

Instant grits   butter   milk or water   salt to taste   pepper to taste   crumbled bacon bits   shredded cheddar cheese. 1   pack   grits   per   person...follow package directions. Garnish ....bacon ... cheese-...easy and tasty. Good   for   your soul.

GOTCHA   SCRAMBLED   EGGS   'N CHEESE

8 eggs lightly beaten   salt to taste   pepper to taste   butter flavored cooking spray   1 C shredded mozzarella cheese   2 diced tomato   4 finely diced green onions with tops   ½ diced green pepper   sprig parsley. Spray skillet with butter flavored cooking spray...add onion.....green pepper.... salt...... pepper... 5-minutes. Add beaten eggs...tomato...cook until eggs are scrambled. Sprinkle cheese on top...microwave until cheese is melted...1- minute...garnish parsley. Needless to say...this is yummy, NOT FOR BOB'S TUMMY

HOT HEAD BISCUITS!

2 C flour   4 t baking powder   1 t salt   2 T shortening   1 C milk. Combine   flour , baking   powder, salt. Blend in shortening   till   mixture   is   coarse.... add   milk,   kneading   gently. Roll out   dough .... Cut with   biscuit- cutter , place   on   greased   baking   sheet.... 10 - 12 minutes...400°.

SAUSAGE GRAVY

2 lb. fresh sausage , fried….crumbled   1 ½ C flour   ½ t salt   ½ t pepper   9 C milk   Add flour to sausage, brown. Stir well…. Add salt… pepper… milk. Heat to boiling…. Reduce heat… simmer, stirring constantly.   Serve and enjoy.   Everything is good with gravy…. Well… maybe not everything!

HOG WILD COUNTRY HAM

½ stick butter   1 ½ pounds Virginia ham cut in ¼ inch slices   ½ cup brewed coffee   ½ cup water   Fresh ground pepper to taste. In a large skillet over moderately high heat, melt butter until the foam subsides; sauté ham in batches until browned; transfer to a platter and keep warm. Deglaze the pan with coffee and water, cooking over high heat for about 2 minutes. Season the gravy with pepper and pour over ham; OR BOB !

A CHILLY CHRISTMAS BUFFET

Christmas Parties..... don't you just love 'em! Everybody smiling behind deceiving pearly whites, mumbling words like, "My God, what did she do to her hair?". Or sweetly, quietly mouthing, "Dear Lord, did she wear her Christmas tree?". And when that icy sippin' stuff makes the guests feel warm and fuzzy all over, the pawin' and pettin' begins. People you have NEVER seen before become your best buddies or whatever, and ALL inhibitions fly out the frosty window panes...Oh, baby Jesus, we thank you for Christmas parties!

With every Christmas party, dear old Bob would merrily add more notches to his pistol and I would become more sick of watching him nibble on pale, ornamental ears of fermented she-guests! You'd think he hadn't eaten in days! Plus, MagicBob's sudden disappearing tricks made everyone think he was part of the entertainment! Oh brother, I couldn't wait for the Christmas Season!!!

Days before the party season began, this not quite 5'3" blonde had been watching every morsel that entered my short system. I really wanted to fit into this waist-cinching, boob-popping Red dress I had purchased just for the merrymaking. Just a little attention from my Wanderlust of a Husband or Whomever...the other town lush, the preacher, the waiter..... would be so gratifying.

We ARE our thoughts you know, so I made merry as I prepared for the first Night of Wonder. Donning my sexy little red dress, decorating my pale ears, and putting on my beautiful new stilettos, I looked in the mirror and thought, "HEY BABY, YOU ARE READY FOR THIS PAR-TEE!!!"

I found Relaxin Bob sitting in front of the larger-than -life screened TV. With bare arms floating in the air, I bopped around in front of the monster, TV that is, and romantically asked, "How do I look?". WRONG as usual! Bob's chill-to-the- bone reply....."What difference does it make, NOBODY'S GONNA LOOK AT YOU ANYWAY!"

Needless to say, I didn't make it to that Par-tee! And one of my beautiful stilettos ended up as a piece of modern art in our entry hall door! As MeanBadBob pulled his jacket from the closet to make Merry, or Helen, or Judy, I took my shoe, threw it as hard as I could, and that skinny, long heel stuck perfectly in the door panel. Of course I left it to remind myself of future stupidity!!! On occasion, during the different Seasons, I decorated the beautiful foot piece with whatever was appropriate for the period. This gave me much pleasure as I thought of the heel almost sticking in the tail-end of the REAL HEEL!

TIPS: Leave your mistakes, particularly if they can be seen….they make for great conversation!
        NEVER ask ANYONE how you look…they usually lie, one way or another…your thoughts are better than anyone
         elses.   TRUST YOURSELF!!!!!

RECIPES FOR:

    ParTee Champagne Punch   Ornamental Cheese Nibbles   Fermented Fruit Combo
        Disappearing Beef KaBOB   Scrumptious Evil Chicken
    Mean Dirty Rice   Heart-of-a-Heel Salad   'What a Knucklehead' Pasta
        Ugly Ducklin' Cake   Red Devil Cake   PW

A CHILLY CHRISTMAS BUFFET

ORNAMENTAL CHEESE NIBBLES
Mix together: 2 sticks butter   2 C flour   Red pepper
2 C grated sharp Cheddar cheese   2 C crispy rice cereal
Shape into balls then flatten with fork.   Bake at 375°
For 10 to 12 minutes. BOB CAN DO SOME NIBBLING
ON THESE LIL GOODIES INSTEAD OF THE LADIES!!

FERMENTED FRUIT COMBO
Drain 1 15 oz can pineapple chunks and save the juice.
Combine the chunks with 3 C cantaloupe or honey dew
Melon balls, and 1 C strawberries.
Mix the pineapple juice with $\frac{1}{4}$ C orange marmalade and
4 to 5 T orange liqueur. Pour over fruit and stir lightly.
Chill the DRUNK fruit for about 1 to 2 hours.

DISAPPEARING BEEF KABOBS
Combine the following to make a marinade:
Juice of 1 $\frac{1}{2}$ lemons   3 T canola oil   1 grated onion $\frac{1}{4}$ t ginger
1 T Teriyaki   1 t salt/pepper   2 t Worcestershire   1 Bay leaf
1 clove crushed garlic   1 t mustard.   Add 3 lbs cubed sirloin and
several whole fresh mushrooms to the marinade for 4 hours.
Meanwhile prepare green, red, or yellow pepper chunks, cherry
tomatoes, and small sweet onions to alternate with the beef and
mushrooms on metal skewers. Grill about 20 minutes brushing
often with marinade. THE COOKING AROMA IS DIVINE!!

PW

SCRUMPTIOUS EVIL CHICKEN
Brown 1 bag skinless chicken filets in hot
oil. Add salt/pepper to taste and 6 to 8
washed and cut-up potatoes. Mix together
1 C orange juice, $\frac{1}{4}$ C brown sugar, 1 t ginger.
Pour over the chicken and simmer 45 minutes.

MEAN DIRTY RICE
Cook 1 lb ground beef with 2 cloves garlic,
2 chopped celery stalks, 1 chopped onion,
1 cored red pepper, and 1 T parsley. Crumble
beef as it cooks. Stir in 1 t salt, $\frac{1}{4}$ t red/black
pepper, 1 T Worcestershire sauce, 1 can beef
broth, 1 C uncooked rice, $\frac{3}{4}$ C water. Simmer
for 30 to 45 minutes.
THIS IS EVEN MEANER THAN BOB!!!

HEART-OF-A-HEEL SALAD
Layer the following in the order given...when
ready to serve, TOSS and YOU GOT IT!
Broken up red tip/iceberg lettuce
1 pkg thawed English peas, cauliflower, broccoli
bunch green onions, shredded carrots
4 hard boiled eggs, pkg REAL bacon bits
Seal with mayonnaise, salad supreme, Parmesan
cheese

'WHAT A KNUCKLEHEAD' PASTA

Cook a 16 oz pkg bow tie pasta accordin' to its directions. Saute then cook the following for 10 minutes:
1 small chopped onion   2 chopped garlic cloves   2 T olive oil   2 cups chopped Plum tomatoes
about 8 oz of sliced fresh mushroom $\frac{1}{2}$ t crushed red pepper $\frac{3}{4}$ t salt
Stir in $\frac{1}{2}$ C whippin' cream   3 oz cream cheese   3 T basil   3 T Romano cheese
Pour over drained bow ties...mix well.....sprinkle with more Romano/Parmesan mix cheese.
KNUCKLEHEAD PERFECTO!

UGLY DUCKLIN CAKE

Blend ALL the following together....Beat 4 minutes....Pour into a floured 9x13 pan.....Top with $\frac{1}{2}$ c brown sugar $\frac{1}{2}$ C pecans.
1 yellow cake mix   1 small pkg lemon instant puddin'   1 16 oz fruit cocktail with syrup
1 C coconut   4 eggs $\frac{1}{4}$ C canola oil
Bake at 325° for about 45 minutes and add the following glaze:
$\frac{1}{2}$ C butter $\frac{1}{2}$ C sugar $\frac{1}{2}$ C evaporated Milk   1 $\frac{1}{2}$ C flaked coconut......cook until sugar is dissolved and then
POUR IT ON JUST LIKE BOB DOES WITH THE LADIES AND WHOEVER ELSE WILL LISTEN TO HIM!!!

RED DEVIL CAKE

Make a Chocolate Devils Food Cake as the directions indicate and ice the dark devil with the following:

Devil Icing

Cream $\frac{1}{4}$ C butter and gradually add 2 C powdered sugar...mixing well.
Add 2 T milk   1 teaspoon vanilla   Enough Red Food coloring to change this yummy white stuff to RED.
A HIT WITH EVERYBODY, EVEN THE DARK DEVIL BOB!

PW

THE CHRISTMAS TREE

Watching from the large bay window, little sparkling eyes gazed upon the snowy driveway, anxiously awaiting their gay ol father to arrive with a large bushy Christmas Tree. Little red-haired Jack and his curly haired sister Ginger had been ever so carefully unwrapping the awesome reindeer ornaments. They simply couldn't wait to don the tree with the joyous, leaping-in-the-air, ceramic likenesses of Santa's magical-hoofed-beasts! Jack was holding the red-nosed one probably because it reminded him of his daddy's beet-red snozzle. Precious Gin was clutchin' the sophisticated Blitzer, never realizing the association to her DaDo BobO.

We three merrymakers were cheerfully anticipating our forthcoming, festive, short-lived tradition of trimming 'ye old needle-shedder'! For the last three Christmas seasons we, rather I, tried making a jolly ritual by preparing a fun, child-oriented, tree-trimmin' dinner, yet scrumptious enough for any partaking adults….. sometimes grandparents, sometimes cheerful friends and neighbors. Preparations were busily underway. I slowly pulled the Hint-of Mint Caramel Brownies from the oven, and thought to myself, " Is there anything more wonderful than the aroma of baking yuletide goodies?" Suddenly I could hear giggles and excitement from my two angels as car lights shone on the glistening pavement. Jack and Gin immediately flew toward the door screaming, "Whez's the twee, whez's the twee?"

As DaddyBob approached, instead of capturing a whiff of mint brownie I caught wind of a hint-of-Spirit and NOT of the Christmas kind!!! The children's joyfulness ceased when they realized there was no tree, only their rosy-cheeked, possum-grinnin' father swaying in the hallway like a wind-swept Spineless Pine!!! I am quite sure OFullOfSpirit Bob had already selected and decorated his full-figured, bushy tree hours earlier……not giving a second thought to our traditional, tree-trimmin night at home. Luckily no guests had been invited to share this year! Through squinted, blood-shot eyes Bob saw my frosty stare, turned around, looked down, and told his disappointed twosome he would be right back with a beautiful tree. The StaggerinStud headed out the door! Acceptant, as only children can be, Jack and Ginger went about dancing to the jolly Christmas tunes.

Hours passed, but we saw NO bushy tree or a tottering father. Joyfully we ate our enchanting morsels dedicated to all the magical Winter characters, including DaddyBob who could disappear like the best of them!!!

Knowing all too well our Christmas tree was still in the stand at the local Kroger store, and Bob was still out visiting with all the other red-nosed, unintended toed-beasts at the Moose Lodge, we dressed in our warmest layered fuzzies and headed out into the Winter Wonderland. The night of tradition was not lost! The last beautiful tree was placed in our yellow station wagon, and what a tree it was! It filled our senses with pine essence, you know that smell that has never left your mind after all these years...that wonderful aroma that replaces an otherwise disastrous situation. We headed home singin' every Yuletide song we could muster, especially Rudolph the RED-NOSED Dado. Oh Joyeux Noel!!!!

TIP: Get real mothers!   Bundle up your precious cherubs and BUY THE TREE YOURSELF!
    Before the outing make up new Christmas songs to old familiar tunes, like:
        O Deceitful Dad to the tune of O Christmas Tree or
        Come Fraudulent Father to the melody of O Come All Ye Faithful, just to name a few. The kiddies are so young they have no idea what they're saying......they just think they're playing a game!!!

PW

RECIPES FOR:

BobaClaus Peppermint Eggnog   Red-Nosed Dado Fruit Punch   Bushy Tree Sours
Lil' Daddy Sweet/Sour Weiners   StaggerinStud Cheese Sausage Balls
Magical Leaping Moose Quiche   Bourbon-Marinated Pork Tenderloin
Winter Wonderland Smashed Potatoes
Spirit-Filled Hint-of-Mint Caramel Brownies with a
      Mountain of Snowball Vanilla Ice cream
Frosty Red/Green Jello Delight

THE CHRISTMAS TREE

LIL' DADDY SWEET/SOUR WEINERS
In a fondue pot, simmer 1 small jar grape jelly and 1 small bottle of yellow mustard...stir to mix well
Cut 2 pkgs of Beef hotdogs into bite-sized pieces and let 'em simmer for 20 to 30 minutes in the sauce.
Keep warm through servin' time.....regular hot dogs are used because they're softer than cocktail wieners.

STAGGERIN' STUD CHEESE SAUSAGE BALLS
WHOOPS! 1 lb. cooked & DRAINED SAUSAGE

Combine the following cheeses with ½ C chopped nuts: 1 4 oz shredded Colby/Monterey cheese
1 3 oz cream cheese   1 6 oz shredded Cheddar cheese
Add: 1 T parsley   ½ tsp Worcestershire   1 T grated onion   2/3 drops hot sauce   sprinkle of garlic salt
Form into bite-size balls and roll in finely chopped nuts.   SO CUTE...PARTICULARLY FOR KIDS.
SO I GUESS BOB'S WILL LIKE EM TOO!

MAGICAL LEAPING MOOSE QUICHE
Mix ALL the ingredients together and pour into little prepared pastry tart crusts...Bake at 325° for about 20 min.:
1 beaten egg   ½ C milk   ½ C shredded Cheddar   ½ C real bacon bits   ½ C cubed ham
2 T chopped green onion   2 T Each/Red pepper/green pepper   salt/pepper to taste

Top with a sprig of parsley and a half cherry tomato.....SO CHRISTMASY...NOT THAT BOB WOULD NOTICE,
BUT THE KIDS WILL!

FROSTY RED/GREEN JELLO DELIGHT
Drain 1 8 oz can of crushed pineapple and 1 10 oz pkg frozen Red Raspberries...reserve the juice...set fruit aside.
Add enough water to the reserve to make 1 C.....bring to a boil then stir into 1 3 oz pkg of Raspberry or cherry jello.
Dissolve...dump in the fruit...1 C applesauce... and ¼ to ½ C chopped pecans.....Let this set for a coupla hours in the frig.
Mix a 3 oz pkg Lime jello as the directions indicate with about ¼ less liquid...when the jello is cooled and almost set,
pour over the red delight.....refrigerate until both layers have set on top one another...pile with whipped topping.
PW

YOU ARE MAGICAL!!!

BOURBON MARINATED PORK TENDERLOIN
For a marinade combine the following: ½ C soy sauce   ½ C teriyaki   ¾ C bourbon   ¼ C Worcestershire
¼ C canola oil   4 crushed garlic cloves   3 T brown sugar   1 tsp ginger   1 tsp salt/pepper

Rinse a 2 to 3 lb pork tenderloin then place in the marinade.....cover.....chill for at least 12 hours
Remove from marinade and discard the liquid. Grill covered on medium heat until all pink is gone   DELICIOUS!

WINTER WONDERLAND SMASHED POTATOES
Make it easy on yourself SINCE YOU LIVE WITH A BOB.....purchase one of those deliciously prepared tubs of
mashed taters and add ya some goodies.....like: ½ C sour cream   ½ C real bacon bits   1 C shredded cheese
3 thinly sliced green onions   ½ C butter   1 T garlic/parsley salt

USE THAT IMAGINATION...THATS WHAT IT'S FOR....LET THE KIDS HELP BUT DEFINITELY NOT BOB.....
NO TELLIN' WHAT HE'D PUT IN, OR WHERE HE'D PUT IT!!!

SPIRIT-FILLED HINT-OF-MINT CARAMEL BROWNIES
Combine the following: ½ C all-purpose flour   ½ C unsweetened cocoa powder   ¼ tsp salt   Mix Well
In another bowl whisk: 3 egg white   4 T applesauce   ¾ C sugar   2 T canola oil   1 ½ tsp vanilla
½ tsp peppermint extract   ¼ C prepared Caramel icing

Combine the two mixtures then pour batter into an 8 inch greased baking pan.....Bake at 350° for about 20 minutes
After baking, while brownies are still warm, SPRINKLE the brownies with the following:
1 small candy cane or other mint candy crushed to a powder and added to ¼ C powdered sugar
Top with a small piece of broken mint   KIDS WILL SQUEAL WITH DELIGHT!

PW

DECISION OLE'

Clare had been preparing a hot and spicy Fiesta dinner for several of their friends, but mostly Bob's colleagues. The occasion….to honor ProBobs new partnership in the business. Damn, if something else hadn't come along making it really hard to leave Scalawago Roberto! He was always so sugar-drippin' humble and professional in front of guests, but a PinheadedBoobBob alone at home, which I must admit, wasn't very often!

Tonight though, I really needed Bob to get home, level-headed and sober as much as possible, so he could retrieve some of his expensive, imported wine from the cellar. Well, that didn't happen! A few moments before the guests were to arrive, Bob strolled in the door arm-in-arm with a HOT, overly aggressive, laughin'-too-loudly, Blonde Bombshel!. Both were reeking of booze and bouncing off the wall!!!

What now, I thought to my wide-opened-mouthed self??? You could have knocked me over with a feather!!! As smooth as a shiny python, Bob also took me by the arm and walked both his blondes to our soft, overstuffed sofa. Sitting between us, he slurringly mumbled, "Well, you two are just gonna have to talk it over and DECIDE WHICH ONE GETS ME…this is jus too much for me to handle!".

He got up, walked off, and both blonde heads dumbfoundedly gazed at one another!!!

TIP: Don't tell Bob when you're givin' him a party! Better yet DO NOT GIVE THE BOOB ANYTHING!!!

RECIPES FOR: PW

Sugar-Drippin Melon Coolers   Smooth Pythons   ProBobs Imported Wines
Seven Layer Scalawago Dip   Holy Guacamole   Hot n Bouncing Crab, Artichoke and Jalapeno
Overstuffed Blonde Potatoes   Tricky Dicky Tamale Chili Pie
PinheadedBoobBob Marinated Flank Steak   Blonde Flan

DECISION OLE

SEVEN LAYER SCALAWAGO DIP
  Getcha' a colorful, Latino casserole dish and layer the following:
    2 cans refried beans with green chilies   2 lbs. Browned and drained lean ground beef   1 pkg Taco seasoning
    1 can Ranch style beans   1 C mayonnaise + 1 C sour cream   1 small can sliced black olives   1 jar picante sauce
    1 ½ C sharp shredded Cheddar cheese + 1 ½ C shredded Monterey Jack cheese   1 bunch chopped green onions

  Cook at 325° for 25 to 30 minutes.   MY DECISION WOULD BE TO EAT THE DIP WITH CORN CHIPS.....
            TO HECK WITH FIGHTIN' OVER BOB   LETS EAT!!!

HOLY GUACAMOLE
  Peel and mash 1 avocado to mix with: 1 ½ T lemon juice   1 T cilantro   2 cloves minced garlic   1 t basil   1 t salt
  Peel and dice another avocado.....fold into the mixture with: ¼ C red pepper   2 T salsa   2 T sliced green onion
MIX EAT AS IS WITH SOUR CREAM TOPPING AND TORTILLA CHIPS OR DOLLOP ONTO SCALAWAGO DIP.....OLE'

HOT 'N BOUNCING CRAB, ARTICHOKE AND JALAPENO
  In a large skillet cook 1 lg cored green pepper. Throw in 2 14 oz cans drained/chopped artichoke hearts,
  2 C mayonnaise, ½ C chopped green onions, ½ C drained/chopped pimento, 1 C parmesan cheese, 1 ½ T lemon juice,
  4 t Worcestershire Sauce, 3 pickled/drained/chopped jalaoeno peppers, 1 t celery salt, 1 lb drained Crabmeat.

Dump beautiful mixture into a buttered baking dish.....sprinkle with 1/3 C sliced almonds.....BAKE at 375° for 30 minutes.
            DEVOUR WITH PITA TRIANGLES AND CHA...CHA...CHA!!!

OVERSTUFFED BLONDE POTATOES

Bake or Microwave 4 or more Yukon potatoes that you have rubbed with oil.
Beat the following together: 1 lg cream cheese   1 mashed avocado   2 T milk   1 T lemon juice   1 T grated onion
When potatoes are done, split and fluff the pulp.....cream the mixture into each potato and top with REAL bacon bits.
THIS IS SOME BLONDE BOMBSHELL.....YUMMY!

TRICKY DICKY TAMALE CHILI PIE

Combine the following in a greased 1 ½ quart casserole: 1 25 oz can chili with beans   1 14 oz can tamales cut in thirds
1 chopped onion   1 or 2 chopped jalepeno peppers

Bake at 400° for 25 minutes.   Combine 1 C corn chips with 1 C shredded Cheddar cheese and 1 peeled/sliced avocado
Sprinkle over the top of the hot casserole and bake 5 or so more minutes.
HOPE BOB GETS A TASTE OF THIS DISH!!!

PINHEADEDBOOBBOBS DRUNK FLANK STEAK

Marinate a 2 lb Flank steak at least 2 hrs, up to 8 hrs, in the following delicious mixture:

¼ C soy sauce	¼ C dry sherry	¼ C teriyaki sauce
¼ C olive oil	2 T grated orange rind	¼ C orange juice
2 chopped cloves garlic	1 T minced fresh ginger	2 t brown sugar

Remove from marinade and Grill on an oil coated grate for 8 to 10 minutes for each side. Dab with marinade as it cooks.
Marinade may be cooked over a medium/high heat until it slightly thickens to be served with the steak.
IF YOU DO THIS RIGHT.....DELICIOUSLY SINFUL!!!

BLONDE FLAN

Mix 1 14 oz can sweetened condensed milk with 1 C water, 3 beaten eggs, and 1 T vanilla.
Melt 1 C sugar in a heavy pan until it turns a caramel color. When it is a liquid, pour sugar into a deep dish
Pie pan. Pour first mixture over the melted sugar. Set in a pan of water and Bake for 30 minutes
or until knife inserted in center comes out clean.

A FANTASTIC DESSERT THAT IS SO QUICK AND EASY.....JUST LIKE BOB.
BUT HE IS NOT FANTASTIC.....ONLY QUICK AND EASY!!!   PW

EASY AS PIE

Blunderin' Bob wanted to go to the Club for the Holiday and partake of the goodies.....good Mary Jane, good Sally Sue, and good old Rhonda with the Red dress on or off! Peyton Place couldn't 'hold a candle' to the Mischievous Nonsense that went on after hours, in the Gents Locker Room!

Thanksgiving morning, Bob the Predictable started his nit-pickin' attitude. After a short time, he finally had worked his way up to a screamin' frenzy!!! "YOU screw-up every occasion with your Goody-Two-Shoes Crap," he hollered. He exited the back door like a raging Bull! Oh well, I had certainly seen this Show before, so, like all good Southern wives would do, I decided to bake Holiday Pies and ALTER BOB'S WARDROBE! Oh what FUN!!!

Every good Seamstress will tell you that a little gadget called a seam-ripper and a pair of nice little, sharp scissors can turn an ordinary pair of pants into a work of Art...maybe. I, very skillfully, nipped the threads in the seat of BobbyBoys favorite trousers and cut neat tiny holes in all the pockets.....a perfect example of when less is more!

Feelin' absolutely euphoric, I baked the most delicious pies ever!

TIP: Do something EVERYDAY to make yourself happy.

RECIPES FOR:

Moon You Pie	Plastered Pumpkin Pie	Holy Terror Pie
Nuts to you pie	Hoppin' Mad Pie	Fudge You Pie

LC

EASY AS PIE

MOON YOU PIE

1 C graham cracker crumbs   2 T sugar   ¼ C melted butter   2 C marshmallows   ½ C milk   ½ t vanilla   1 C whipped cream   2 squares semisweet chocolate................ save a few marshmallow for garnish. Combine graham cracker crumbs, sugar, and butter; press into bottom and up sides of pie plate. Melt marshmallows in milk over low heat, stirring frequently. Cool. Add vanilla; fold in whipped cream and chocolate. Pour into crumb crust; chill thoroughly. Add marshmallows as garnish. You ain't seen nothing yet !

PLASTERED PUMPKIN PIE

1 (9-inch) pie crust   2 eggs, slightly beaten   1 C brown sugar   ½ t ginger   ½ t cinnamon   ½ t nutmeg   1 ¾ C pumpkin   ½ C milk   ½ cup cream   5 T rum   ½ C raisins. Bake pie crust at 400 ° for 5 minutes. Combine eggs, brown sugar, spices, pumpkin, milk cream and rum. Stir in raisins. Bake at 350 ° for 1 hour or until knife comes out clean. PUNCH-DRUNK - PUMPKIN- HEAD misses another goody !

HOLY TERROR PIE

1 21 oz can apple pie filling   1 (9-inch) pie crust   12 caramel candies   ¼ cup butter   1 T lemon juice   2 T milk 1 ½ C whipped cream. Pour apple pie filling into prepared 9 inch pie shell. Combine caramels, butter, lemon juice and milk in saucepan; heat over low heat stirring constantly until smooth and caramels are melted. Pour over apples. Bake at 400 ° until brown, 25 – 30 minutes.   Just what the doctor ordered.

NUTS TO YOU PIE

1 (9-inch) unbaked pie crust   2/3 C sugar   ½ t salt   1 C dark corn syrup   1/3 C creamy peanut butter   3 eggs   1 C salted peanuts. Beat sugar, salt, corn syrup, peanut butter and eggs; stir in peanuts. Pour into pie crust. Bake at 375° for 40 – 50 minutes until golden brown... cool slightly... refrigerate.   NUTTIN' BETTER !

HOPPIN MAD PIE

2 large containers whipped cream   1 ½ C sliced peaches   1 ½ C Mandarin oranges   1 ½ C chunk pineapple   1 can condensed milk   1/3 C lemon juice   2 graham cracker pie crusts. Drain fruit and cut up peaches. Mix whipped cream, condensed milk and lemon juice. Add fruit. Pour into 2 pie crusts and chill. AIN'T NOTHIN HOPPIN BUT THE PEAS IN THE POT AND THEY WOULDN'T BE HOPPIN IF THE WATER WASN'T HOT!

FUDGE YOU PIE

1 C butter   1 C sugar   2 eggs   ½ C flour   1 t vanilla   1 square... unsweetened- chocolate. Cream butter. Add sugar, eggs, one at a time. Add flour, vanilla. Melt chocolate and add to mixture. Pour into glass pie plate. Bake 30 minutes at 325°. The unusual part of this pie is it does not have a crust. CRUSTY BOB IS ENOUGH CRUST FOR ANYONE !

LC

ELVIS BLUES

Jack and Gin loved their little songs they played on their red record player. The nursery rhymes would be so fondly listened to over and over again until they had them all memorized. The precious twosome would dance and sing off key so loudly just to outdo the other. One happy morning Jack and Ginger found some old boxes under the stairs that I hadn't gone through in years. They were delighted when they came to one filled with black, small discs….my old 45 record collection. Most had the Motown label but a few had RCA and the name of Elvis Presley. OH MY GOSH, my heart started to flutter as the three of us ran to the little red player. We wiggled, we squealed with delight, and I fell in love all over again, at the same time my four and five year old discovered THE KING OF ROCK n ROLL!

This was sure a far cry from the nursery rhymes! No more Baa Baa Black Sheep! All Jack, Gin and their Alright Mama wanted now was to hear from the REAL BLACK SHEEP himself…..Elvis Presley!!!!! So, we hopped into the car and made a mad dash for the Record Shop in The Village. Walking into the place was like walking into a concert. It was poster filled and giant cardboard likenesses stood right before us. There HE was, posed in a tight white jumpsuit, blue suede shoes , with sunglasses as big as the moon. Each child ran to him screamin, "is dis him", "is dis EVIS"?

Suddenly, out of nowhere, there stood this tall, slim, red-haired salesgirl. She had obviously been watchin' us from afar, just waitin to strike a Heartbreak Hotel on us! All sweet and gooey she said, "Whach'al little people need?" I could swear she was also including me! And you know how intuition just makes ya shiver sometimes, well, the blonde hairs on my head practically stood on end! I immediately knew that Red, the Viper, was not wantin' to sell us Elvis records!!! This tall Carrot-top was Our Enemy! I was overtaken with the GI blues!!!!!

My Suspicious Mind was racin' as Jack and Gin went about happily looking through the Spinnin' Disc Shop. Sure enough, the Scarlet Harlot bent down and whispered, "You are Robert's wife, right?" I wanted to answer, "No, I'm just the housekeeper and babysitter," but darn, I was too curious!!! This was a new one! "I really need to talk to you," Red proceeded to hiss. I looked straight into those cold dark eyes, paid for Elvis, and said, "Sure, that will be a real treat….how about 2:00?" I knew my two Hound Dogs would be worn out by then.

Lunch with the King was awesome….we rocked, we rolled, we shimmied, we shook like something on a fuzzy tree, and we sang until naptime when I had to face the 'Bob Thing'.

Sure enough, the phone rang at 2:00 on the nose. I sat speechless as I listened to the venomous tales the Copperheaded Queen was spittin' into my ear! It seems Red and her family were involved in a lawsuit, hired Bob to solve their problems, and fallen IN LOVE WITH THE SNAKE-IN-THE-GRASS!!!! How romantic!!! I mean the whole family was infatuated with the charmin' low-life. Scaly Red's parents also entered the phone conversation and informed me of Bob's undying love for their offspring. They couldn't wait for him to become their son-in-law since, "ya'll will be divorcing soon anyway, right?", said Mother Serpent. They were tickled pink to soon be, "havin' a lawya in the family," said Daddy Reptile!

True, there had been no Peace in our Valley for sometime, but I wasn't about to let THEM know. I thanked these lovely home wrecking Vipers for the enlightening conversation, then just sat mesmerized.

If adultery was a crime, All the jailhouses would be rockin' with BOB'S!
Oh Daddy, Daddy was sure gonna be cryin' tonight! That is, if he managed to SLITHER home.

TIPS: Always have a defense ready, like a good heavy rake or Moth Balls when vermin invade your territory.
Listen to any Elvis record right now and you'll be in love in seconds!

RECIPES FOR:

Peanut Butter and BoBanana Sandwiches   Infatuating Jelly Donuts   Tickled Pink Lemonade
Carrot-topped Tomatoes   Jailhouse Rockin Macaroni 'n Cheese
GI Blue Shimmying Jello in Cantaloupe halves   Hound Dogs in Crescent Rolls   Copperhead Cookies
Sweet n Gooey Red Viper Ice Cream   Bob Things and Scarlet Harlots for the Alright Mama   PW

ELVIS BLUES

PEANUT BUTTER AND BOBANANA SANDWICHES
This is rather simple but soooooo good!
Just take your favorite Peanut Butter...spread on soft
White bread...cut thin slices of banana over the PB...
Smear a thin coat of Grape jelly on other White slice...
Cover PB and 'nanas for *SOME GOOD EATIN!*

CARROT-TOPPED TOMATOES
Half a nice juicy ripe tomato.
Smear with Mayonnaise.
Salt lightly. Sprinkle with shredded
fresh carrots and shredded yellow cheese. *COOL!!!*

INFATUATING JELLY DONUTS
You don't need to make these....you cant get
any better than your local Donut Shop.
ELVIS AND BOB JUST LOVE 'EM.

HOUND DOGS IN CRESCENT ROLLS
Easy as Pie! Separate a pkg refrigerated
crescent rolls...separate...roll 'em out.
Smear with mustard and place half a hotdog on
top...roll 'em up and plop the lil dogs in the oven
like the directions say. O.K.!!!

JAILHOUSE ROCKIN MACARONI 'N CHEESE
Cook Bow Tie Macaroni as directions indicate...drain. Mix together: 2 C Cottage cheese   1 C Sour cream   1 egg
$\frac{3}{4}$ tsp salt   dash black pepper   8 oz shredded Sharp American cheese   dash of paprika
and the cooked Bow Ties. Bake in a 9 inch baking dish at 350° for 30 to 45 minutes. KIDS AND BOB'S LOVE IT !!!

GI BLUE SHIMMYING JELLO IN CANTALOUPE HALVES
Half a good melon and scoop out the seeds (dry 'em/plant 'em...it'll give BOB SOMETHING ELSE TO DO!!!)
Prepare a lg pkg of Blue jello with a little LESS water than calls for...pour into halves that you've set into bowls to
keep it sittin straight. When firm, cut the halves into quarters and dobble with a scoop of prepared Vanilla puddin.
THREE DESSERTS IN ONE.....WHOOPIE!

TICKLED PINK LEMONADE
Mix 1 small frozen pink lemonade/1small frozen limeade/1 small frozen orange juice...blend with a large citrus peach
soda...Pour over lots of crushed ice in a tall, skinny glass with a straw...also throw in a slice of fresh peach or pink
grapefruit.
COOL AND REFRESHING FOR EVERYBODY...MAYBE YOU CAN COOL DOWN BOBO!

COPPERHEAD COOKIES
Combine all the following with 1 C creamed butter: ½ C brown sugar   2 ¼ C all-purpose flour   ½ C chopped pecans
Divide dough in half and chill for 1 hour. Pull plugs from dough after chillin' then roll on waxed paper to resemble
Snakes...Bake at 300° until golden...watch carefully for uneven baking. When cool decorate your snakes with
tubes of Red decorator icing...GOTTA WATCH 'EM...THEY'LL BE GONE QUICKLY....JUST LIKE BOB!

SWEET 'N GOOEY RED VIPER ICE CREAM
Soften your very favorite store-bought Strawberry Ice Cream. Dump a pkg or two of little, long,
    different colored jelly-belly snakes into the soften cream. Stir to evenly distribute the snakies
    so everybody is sure to get at least one Viper. Refreeze. Serve and JUST WATCH THE FUN SURPRISE!

PW

FARMHOUSE RENDEVOUS

Healthy, Wealthy, not-so-Wise SneakyBob came up with what he considered a fantastic plan! He quickly pulled his driver, bodyguard, and confidant-in-crime, BillieBob, in on the idea. BobbyBoy was getting caught at his illicit games, so he had to come up with something new, safer, and a distance from town. He had found an old Farmhouse for sale that would do just fine for rendezvousing! He was bored with paying for his latest mistake, and was ready for ACTION!!!

The antic that landed BulldogBob in the doghouse for months was when he decided to install a private door from his office to the alleyway behind his building. That worked fabulously for a time....he had his female clients Coming and Goin all day long. But, some good secretary told somebody elses good secretary, that told a friend of JolieAnn, Bob's good wife!

Wow, she quickly put a STOP to that Swingin' Door Thing! JolieAnn parked on the street next to the alleyway, and sure enough, here came Floozy, whose perfume was so strong you could smell it a mile away! She turned into the narrow Walk of Sin, knocked once, and entered the Den of Iniquity. JolieAnn just pulled right into the short drive, blocked the door, and waited. From experience, she knew it wouldn't be long! Soon enough, the AlleyCat, with Bob pettin her all over, tried to enter her natural environment. A cat fight ensued like that alley had never before seen, and RuffledUp Bob ended up in the doghouse! The Swingin door ceased to swing...it was bricked over the next day!

Bob was not about to go through that again, so the Farmhouse was bought and placed in the name of BillieBob. This way RomeoRobert could see his new 'squeeze,' an out-of-towner, any time he wanted. She could even set up 'shop' there whenever she wanted, unless of course, RomeoBob wanted to cheat on the new one, as well as wifey!!! He would have to play the visiting card just right....but hey, Bob was slick....he thought!

Well, 'things' rolled right along at the new, old Farmhouse just like the hay that was still rolled in the field beside the house. BillieBob would just sit and swing and giggle on his big, pretend front porch and watch out for the likes of JolieAnn or a few husbands from around the area that would like to have a piece of this JackASS! The cute little out-of-towner would make great meals for Bob and give him a fantastic 'roll in the hay'! But, this affair was becoming way too comfortable and mighty routine. BillieBob tried warning his BossMan, but the BM didn't want to listen! He would say, "Oh, this is a well-kept secret...no way anybody is gonna find out this one!!!". How on Earth could this Bob be so wealthy...he wasn't too smart!!! There had been so many Bobcatchins', he belonged in the Pound, and this episode was not going to be any different! A screw-up was in the making!

In a small town you don't have to say or do much before people start getting suspicious or putting two and two together! Particularly when it came to an illicit Bigshot like BossMan Bob. Little Ms Out-of-Towner was getting way too visible and friendly with the shoppers and checkers at the local grocery store and pharmacy. Names were dropped at the wrong place at the wrong time, and THAT IS ALL SHE WROTE!!! Just the RIGHT day, there stood JolieAnn soaking up all the muddy water! She followed Ms Prissy out to the county and saw the out-of-towner turn up a dirt road to an old Farmhouse. By damn if it didn't look like crazy BillieBob just swingin on the front porch! Luckily Prissy's car was a diversion, and the Good Wife took off. She now knew where all that mud was comin' from on Bob's big ass car! She would be back!!!

Fed up and totally disgusted, JolieAnn reached in her panty drawer and pulled out her cold, black, stubby .38 revolver that just laid in wait for the right culprit, just like her sexy black panties waitin' for the right moment!. Back at the Farmhouse, all the Pretenders were busy doin' their thing...Prissy cookin' her great After-Sex Spaghetti, WorthlessBob waitin, on the Pot I might add, to eat the great After-Sex Spaghetti, and BillieBob sittin on his pretend porch, swinging and being 'lookout'.

 Like a bat-out-of-Hell, a huge Black Car pulled to the front of the Farmhouse, practically takin BillieBob's pretend porch with it, and throwing dust clear across the hay field! JolieAnn had but one passenger...the cold, black .38, and she was going to use it!!! BillieBob jumped off that pretend swing as fast as his big body could take him, all the while screamin to his BM, "Get outta there Bossman, get outta there...she's packin'!". BM pulled up his britches as fast as he could and ran for the back door...the out-of-towner just stood in bewilderment, her mouth dropping down like she was catchin' flies over the After-Sex Spaghetti pot! BillieBob stood in front of the new, old Farmhouse door, stutterin' as JolieAnn screamed, "Where is that low-down Jackass? This is IT...THIS IS THE LAST TIME!".

BillieBob assumed his BM just kept on runnin' and didn't stop, but NO, Bob hid behind the first big ol hayroll he came to. Meanwhile Prissy had not moved, and JolieAnn just kept screamin, "Where is He BillieBob...if you don't tell me I AM GONNA SHOOT YOUR SORRY JACKASS!!!". BillieBob raised his shaking, hairy arm and pointed around the corner to the hayroll, not knowing Bob was behind it! JolieAnn took a fast aim and began shooting as many bullets the little black gun could hold. Of course, and Thank God for JolieAnn, the thick roll buffered the shots, saving Worthless Bob's Jackass, but scaring him into the next world...almost!!!

JolieAnn stepped into the new, old Farmhouse, gave the out-of-towner a Hellish stare, and told her if she so much as smells that sorry, After-Sex spaghetti anywhere in that county, she would NEVER live to make it again! As for BillieBob, JolieAnn pushed him right off his pretend porch, smack into a big dust patch, choking him half to death!!! She turned and slowly left the property, leaving only a trail of dust, and never looking back.

BillieBob got him his new, old Farmhouse in the deal...he didn't have to pretend anymore! The out-of-towner NEVER came back to that county, much less NEVER made her famous spaghetti again. JolieAnn threw that cold, black .38 revolver deep into the next county's river...she got scared of herself! As for ShakenUpBob, maybe he learned a lesson about being faithful, but rumor still has him sneakin' around pulling all kinds of deals, with all kinds of out-of-towners and in-towners!!!

TIPS: Pack ya a gun...even if its a pretend one! Keep ya some bricks and mortar around...you might have to seal up a whole room!!!

RECIPES FOR:

ShakenUpBobitinis   Swingin'Door Things
AlleyCat Dip   RuffledUpBob Chips
Cold Black Olives
After-Sex Spaghetti   Shots-in-the-Hayroll Slaw   Out-of-Towner Grilled Garlic Bread
Dusty BillieBob Brownies   PW

FARMHOUSE RENDEVOUS

ALLEYCAT DIP
Add all together and bake in a pretty lil baking/servin dish: at 350° for 20 minutes

!/2 C drained salad Olive pieces ¼ C real bacon bits 1 14 oz can drained/chopped Artichoke hearts
1 C mayonnaise 1 C parmesan cheese ½ C shredded Cheddar cheese

RUFFLEDUPBOB CHIPS
Evenly pour a bag of ruffly potato chips on a baking sheet. Sprinkle with:

A seasoning salad mix a little dashin' of a dry Italian salad mix a good shake of Parmesan cheese

Bake at 350° for about 10 minutes then dip into the Alleycat dip.....THIS IS A WILD THING...LIKE BOB!

COLD BLACK OLIVES
Drain 1 lg can of pitted black olives.....Place back in the dry jar and cover with 1 small bottle Worcestershire.....
Marinate for 3 days.....pour sauce off and serve

AFTER-SEX SPAGHETTI
Cook 1 12 oz pkg Linguine pasta as directions indicate.....drain and return to cookin' pot.....set aside
Drain 2 6 ½ oz cans Clam (reserve the juice)......Melt 1 T butter with ¼ C olive oil in a lg skillet.....add 8 oz sliced mushroom
And 3 cloves garlic......saute' 5 minutes then add the clams ½ C white wine 2 T chopped basil 2 T Italian seasonin'
¼ tsp fresh black pepper ¼ tsp red pepper.....Mix all together including the reserved clam juice and cook 5 minutes.....
Add pasta.....stir /toss and cover with grated parmesan cheese DELICIOUS ANYTIME...EVEN AFTER SEX!

SHOTS-IN-THE-HAYROLL SLAW
Combine all the following together then cover/chill at least 1 hour: 1 lg finely chopped bag of slaw 1 chopped onion
1 lg chopped green pepper 1 C chopped pimento-stuffed olives 1 C vinegar 1 C olive oil ½ C dill pickle relish
1 tsp sugar 1 tsp celery salt 1 tsp garlic salt ½ tsp salt/pepper MORE THAN 1 HOUR MIGHT BE NEEDED! PW

OUT-OF-TOWNER GARLIC BREAD

Rub the side of a loaf of good French bread with a clove of garlic.....slice lengthwise down the middle and cover
With ½ stick melted butter.....sprinkle with lemon pepper/garlic parsley salt/basil and Parmesan cheese.....
Place in oven or on grill until hot and crispy

DUSTY BILLIEBOB BROWNIES

Melt ½ C butter with a 12 oz bag of Butterscotch bits......remove from heat and beat 4 eggs and ¼ C brown sugar
into the mixture until it is fluffy......Sift in 1 ½ C all-purpose flour   1 ¼ tsp salt   1 tsp baking powder
and 2 C chopped nuts of your choice.....pour into a greased 15 X 10 X 1 inch pan.....bake at 350° for 25 minutes
Cool.....Cut into squares then dust all over with powdered sugar

FAREWELL LUNCHEON

Since the Jennibeth incident, of course, like a good Southern woman, I decided to give MY GOOD BESTEST FRIEND EVER a So Long, Arriverderci, Hasta Luego, Au Revoir, See Ya Later Alligator Luncheon. Again, like a good Southerner, checking on her genteel etiquette, I checked my 'Magnolia Deep South Party Book' for the appropriateness of my guest list. It stated, and I quote, "If a certain individual is of a distasteful nature, exclude them from your gathering."

Therefore, Jennibeth WAS NOT invited to her own Country Club Luncheon. What a shame!!! It was FABULOUS!!!!

TIP: Ladies, stick with acquaintances...screw GOOD BESTEST FRIENDS EVER!
   Be sure to check with your own Best Ever Southern Party Book before inviting anyone to your next
   Ho Down!

RECIPES FOR:

Punchbowl Scorpions   JenniBlues

So Long Honey Chips

See Ya Later Alligator Bites   Best Ever Sweet Lil Ho Crab Cakes   Arriverderci Floozy Cucumber Rounds
Pickled Jezzies   Deep Fried Jenni Cheese Sticks
Creamed Jezebel Chicken on Toast Triangles   Deadly Friendship Rice   Au Revoir Asparagus
Jezebel Sauce

FABULOUS Magnolia Chocolate Delight
Deep South Coffee   PW

FAREWELL LUNCHEON   PW

SO LONG HONEY CHIPS
Combine the following in a jar with a tight top: 2 T sugar   1 tsp salt   1 tsp paprika   1 tsp mustard
$\frac{1}{4}$ tsp pepper $\frac{1}{4}$ C lemon juice $\frac{3}{4}$ C salad oil   1/3 C HONEY
$\frac{1}{2}$ tsp scraped onion   1 tsp celery seed
After mixin', shake vigorously until well blended. Pour enough of this dressin' into a long pan . Place great tastin'
Wheat Crackers in the dressin, coating by turnin' from side to side. Bake at 225° for about 1 hr., turning often.
UNUSUAL LIKE BOB BUT MUCH BETTER TASTIN!

BEST EVER SWEET LIL' HO' CRAB CAKES
Saute 1 lg cored, finely chopped red bell pepper and $\frac{1}{2}$ medium onion in 2 T butter.
Add   1 C crushed saltine crackers $\frac{1}{2}$ C mayonnaise   2 tsp seafood seasoning   2 tsp Worcestershire
and Mix: 1 beaten egg $\frac{3}{4}$ tsp mustard $\frac{1}{2}$ tsp your favorite Hot sauce   1 lb drained, shredded-like Crabmeat
Shape into small patties and Cook the lil cuties in: $\frac{1}{2}$ T butter and $\frac{1}{2}$ T canola oil for 4 or 5 minutes on each side.

ABSOLUTELY FINE PARTICULARLY TOPPED WITH THE FOLLOWING SAUCE.
Mix together and chill for at least 30 minutes:
2 C mayonnaise $\frac{1}{4}$ C favorite Creole mustard   2 finely chopped garlic cloves   2 T chopped basil
1 T lemon juice   2 tsp paprika $\frac{3}{4}$ tsp coarse black pepper

ARRIVERDERCI FLOOZY CUCUMBER ROUNDS
Stir until blended: 1 3 oz pkgs cream cheese $\frac{1}{4}$ C milk   2 T blue cheese salad dressin mix
Spread on store-bought Crostinis or your favorite small bread rounds. Top with a thin slice of cucumber and stuffed olive.

LOVE THESE LIL DARLINGS.....GREAT WITH CHAMPAGNE TOO!

PICKLED JEZZIES Pour off liquid from 1 16 oz jar Large Green Olives....reserve ½ the liquid. Combine liquid with: 1/3 C olive oil, 1 T minced garlic, ½ tsp oregano. Pour this over the bottled olives and refrigerate for 24 hours before servin.

DEEP FRIED JENNI CHEESE STICKS
Cube a 6 oz block of Gruyere cheese and dip them into 2 well-beaten eggs. Dredge them into ¾ C all-purpose flour.
   Dip again in egg then into 1 ½ C fine crushed dry breadcrumbs. Press firmly into the crumbs so they stick.
   Chill on waxed paper for 30 minutes. Deep fry the lil coated cubes in very hot oil until golden brown. Drain and serve.

SEE YA LATER ALLIGATOR BITES
You can purchase frozen alligator pieces at most good grocery stores now a days. Marinate the pieces for about 1 hour in the following:
   1 can evaporated milk   2 beaten eggs   ½ tsp black pepper/½ red pepper   1 ½ tsp garlic powder
   1 ½ tsp chili powder   ½ tsp Accent   1 tsp basil   1 tsp thyme   1 tsp salt

After marinating, dredge in flour, then finely crushed breadcrumbs.....fry in deep fryer until golden brown and crispy.
DANGEROUSLY DELICIOUS WHEN SERVED WITH JEZEBEL SAUCE.

JEZEBEL SAUCE
Mix the following and refrigerate .....GREAT with ALL meats.
   1 10/12 oz jar pineapple preserves   1 10/12 oz jar apple jelly   1 6 oz bottle horseradish
   1 tsp black pepper   1 ½ oz can dry mustard
A GIFT FROM THE SHAMELESS WOMAN HERSELF!!!

DEADLY FRIENDSHIP RICE
Cook 2 C Brown Rice. Combine: 1 C Italian Salad Dressin'   2 T Soy sauce   1 ½ tsp sugar Add to cooked rice.
   Cover and Chill. Once chilled, fold in the following: 1 bunch chopped green onions   ½ C cooked/crumbled bacon
½ lb fresh spinach cut into thin slices...ENJOY!

PW

CREAMED JEZEBEL CHICKEN

Cook 5/6 lbs. of chicken or turkey breasts and cut into 1 inch pieces (about 4 C). Mix the following to pour over chicky:

3 T butter   8 T all-purpose flour   2 C chicken broth   2 C light cream or milk

Salt/pepper to taste   1 tsp dry mustard   ½ tsp garlic/parsley powder   ½ tsp sugar

¼ tsp nutmeg   1/8 tsp cayenne pepper   ½ tsp paprika   4 chopped hard-boiled eggs

1 small can water chestnuts (drained)   ½ C Sherry

Mix well with the chicken and bake at 325° for about 30 to 45 minutes or until bubbly….Serve over Toast Triangles…

A SAD, BAD TRIANGLE THAT OLD JENNIBETH CREATED…BAD, BAD JEZEBEL JENNI!!!!!

AU REVOIR ASPARAGUS

Melt together: 2 T butter   1 T flour   1 10 oz can cream mushroom soup   2 C shredded Cheddar

Meantime, in a 10 X 6 baking dish, layer: 1 sliced boiled egg   1 15 oz C asparagus spears   ½ the cream mixture

Repeat the layering with: another sliced boiled egg   another 15 oz C asparagus   the other half of cream mixture

SOUNDS REALLY GOOD!   Sprinkle with ½ C buttered bread crumbs and Bake at 325° for 30 minutes.

FABULOUS MAGNOLIA CHOCOLATE DELIGHT

Mix the following together to spread in the bottom of a rectangular baking pan:

1 C flour   ½ C tiny chocolate morsels   1 stick butter   1 cup finely chopped pecans   Bake until LIGHTLY brown.

Beat together until smooth: 1 8 oz cream cheese   1 C Vanilla whipped cream   1 C powdered sugar Spread over 1st layer.

Beat together: 2 small pkg Chocolate puddin   3 C milk Spread over 2nd layer

Top with loads of: whipped cream   chocolate shavings   chopped pecans

SERVE WITH DEEP SOUTH COFFEE OR COFFEE TO YOUR DELIGHT, CAUSE JENNIBETH IS GOIN BYE-BYE!!!
PW

FISHY BUSINESS

Business always came first with ol Breadwinner Bob. He was dedicated to his profession and his group of Merry Men. A road trip with the 'boys' was the ultimate high.....and believe me, THEY ALL WERE!!!

Bob's Company sent the over-achievers on a Wild Weekend Fishin' Trip to the Ozarks......Sporty Bob GOT HOOKED!!! The next week, Ma Bell was ringin' off the wall with late night hang-ups. Giggles and sniggers would start around midnight and kept on keeping on until I told Dixie Girl 'how the cow ate the cabbage.' You see, Dixie Pixie had left ol HillBilly Bobber with a gift that keeps on givin'.....needless to say, he was under-the-weather and all strung-out until the antibiotics kicked in.

I continued to slice 'n dice delicious, scrumptious meals for the family circle. We devoured the fresh Lake Trout from Bob's latest adventure and thoroughly enjoyed the Lemon Pasta with Avocado and vine ripe Tomatoes. Yummy! Poor Robert had left his appetite in Arkansas, and I just couldn't prepare a thing to satisfy his craving and desire for SOME SPECIFIC FOOD GROUP! Oh well, one day UP, the next day DOWN.....such is Life!

TIP: Fish or cut bait!

RECIPES FOR:

Floozy Fresh Lake Trout

Rapid River Salad

Love-In Lemon Pasta with Avocado and Tomato

Squash You Casserole

Raisin Hell Nut Pie with Mounds of Homemade Ice Cream

White Wine Aplenty

LC

FLOOZY FRESH LAKE TROUT

1 pound trout fillets   ¼ C butter   2 T lemon juice   ¼ C flour   ½ t salt   1/8 t white pepper   Paprika. Combine butter and lemon juice. Mix flour, salt and white pepper. Dip fish into butter mixture; coat with flour mixture. Place in ungreased square baking dish; pour butter over fish; sprinkle with paprika. Bake at 350 ° for 25 – 30 minutes, until fish flakes easily with fork.   UNDER -THE - WEATHER   ROBERT COULDN'T EAT A BITE…TOO BAD!

RAPID RIVER SALAD

1 medium cucumber thinly sliced   ½ C thinly sliced red onion   ½ C plain low-fat yogurt   4 packets artificial sweetener   ½ t salt   ½ t pepper   2 large tomatoes sliced.   Combine cucumber and onion slices in a bowl. Combine remaining ingredients and add to mix. Toss. Serve immediately over tomato slices. I   enjoyed slicing MEDIUM SIZE   cucumbers,   it was great therapy.

LOVE-IN LEMON PASTA WITH AVOCADO AND TOMATO

1 16 oz package thin spaghetti   2 ripe (firm) avocado   2 ripe (firm) tomato   1 small can sliced black olives   1 ½ T olive oil   1 ½ T butter   garlic salt to taste   lemon pepper to taste   juice of one lemon. Peel and dice avocado and tomato. Add garlic salt… lemon pepper….stir gently. Melt butter… add olive oil.. Prepare pasta according to package directions…drain. Combine ALL ingredients….toss lightly…garnish with fresh rosemary and shredded parmesan cheese. GRUMPY WENT OVERBOARD FOR THIS CULINARY DELIGHT !

SQUASH YOU CASSEROLE

1 lb. cooked squash (3 pkg. frozen)   2 eggs, beaten   ¼ C evaporated milk   2 T sugar   ½ stick butter   1 small onion, chopped   ½ lb sharp grated cheese   ½ pkg slivered almonds   10 crackers.   Layer squash, cheese and almonds in greased casserole dish. Mix butter with crumbs from 10 crackers and spread on top. Bake at 350 ° for 30 minutes.

RAISIN HELL NUT PIE WITH MOUNDS OF HOMEMADE ICE CREAM

2 (9-inch) unbaked pie crusts   3 C raisins   6 C water   ¾ C sugar   2 T cornstarch   pinch salt   1 egg   1 C chopped pecans. Cook raisins with 6 cups water until softened; cool. Mix together sugar, cornstarch and salt; add to raisin mixture. Add egg; beat well. Bring mixture to a boil; pour into crust. Cut remaining pie crust into strips and use to form lattice over top of raisin mixture. Bake at 350 ° for 1 hour.
1 (14 oz) can sweetened condensed milk   2/3 C chocolate-flavored syrup   2 C whipping cream, whipped. In large mixing bowl, combine sweetened condensed milk and syrup. Fold in whipped cream. Pour into 9 x 5-inch loaf pan or other 2 quart container; cover. Freeze 6 hours or until firm.

WHITE WINE APLENTY

3 liters citrus soda   1 large jar cherries and juice   1 bottle lime juice   1 large can frozen lime concentrate   1 ½ bottles cheap vodka   1 bottle cheap white wine   1 large bag ice. Stir all ingredients in cheap cooler using a large boat paddle which can be used later to keep Bob off of you!

LC

A FISHY GOURMET BEACH LUNCH

Twilight on the beach is just magnificently romantic!   But, the wrong mix can certainly turn-the-tide! One particular summer twilight, I had seen just about all the sunsets I could stand...ALONE again, naturally. You see, my RuthlessAttorneyBob husband, his personal secretary Melba, and my very Blonde self, snaked our way through the Southern states to the Emerald Coast and Crystal Beaches of Destin, Fl.   SouthernBoy Bob and I had baked our bodies there every summer since our honeymoon five years ago, draggin' a lot of unnecessary stuff, but NEVER a secretary!!!

But, of course, this was a BUSINESS TRIP to purchase land for some high and mighty client. Therefore, BimboMelba was included, or so they both agreed. I thought it was an invasion of our privacy, even though Bob and I hadn't experienced 'anything private' in a long time!!!! ProBob actually expected me to swallow this fishy tale, hook, line, and sinker! And, of course I did...a little bit! I was suspecting something smelly...the man had not been called 'SMELLY' Bobby for nothing! But, why miss a trip to frolic in the sun and surf, right? Nobody thinks about wrinkles when you're that young and STUPID and Blonde! Plus, I really NEVER believed the man was having Sex with EVERYBODY BUT ME!!!

We settled into the 'Sun and Stuff' Motel and immediately there was WAY TOO MUCH laughter and boozing-it-up between SurfinBob and MooninMelba (the womans pants were always tooooo tight for her bigass booty so you always thought you were getting mooned when she bent over). Their tune rang of racy conversations and in-your-face laughter, but of course, that was always explained as 'inside deal jokes'. Inside WHAT was all I was thinking! Naiveté was quickly turning to caution, and I was beginning to realize my presence was nothing by a ruse. And in my minds eye, and after only five years of marriage, what husband would pursue or continue an affair right in front of his Dumb Blonde wife???? BOB WOULD, COULD, and DID!!!

During the first morning, I was dropped off at the beach to the rhetoric of, "we're going down the beach aways to check out the land and we'll be back inna coupla hours." So, with my cooler brimming over with fantastic beach-eattin' goodies, I joined one million other beach goers, two of them NOT being Melba and Bob!!! Stupidly I thought I would be joined later by my fun loving husband and 'draggin' ass' Melba. That was not the case!!

A coupla hours turned to amany hours. Scorched, parched, and a little marinated, I fumbled my way to the 'Stuff' Motel. Trudging through the hot sand, pullin' my trusty cooler, I could only think of finding a Good Shark Fisherman! I knew exactly where to find good, fresh bait! And of course, I hadn't touched the scrumptious beach lunch, only the beach liquids....in my stupid mind's eye again, I actually thought they might be there at any moment, OK???? I stuck my well-planned beach goodies in the frig for the night, only to be packed back into my good old cooler in the morning. Surely THEY would partake of the luscious beach lunch tomorrow.....but in my heart I know the partaking would be of another pleasure!!!

The two beach BUMS dragged their way in after twilight, just as pale as when they left and reeking of SEX ON THE BEACH, the luscious, ludicrous drink of course! But I was COOL, even though I was burning INSIDE and OUT! No questions asked...no explanation given! Sleep came easy even if I did have to sleep with Melba????? Bob snored away in his own bed.... Strange!!!

The next day saw a repeat performance, but when I stumbled in with my uneaten lunch again, I found NOTHING! EVERYTHING WAS GONE!!!!! Everything except my stuff in a little pile.   They had left me...I mean THEY HAD REALLY LEFT ME with no way home and way too little money. I found myself ALONE, at the 'Sun and Stuff' Motel in Destin, FL to fin for myself! I plopped myself on the floor, wanting to cry but broke out in hysterical laughter. I was actually relieved.... The charade was over and I could finally eat my gourmet lunch and finish off the fine red wine punch. Thank God for great little, old coolers and a secret stash of $$$$$!

TIP: Make sure you have a really great rolling cooler in case your food must last FOREVER and you have to walk quite a ways....scorched.....like on a beach. When the 'secretary' goes anywhere with you and HubbyBob, just know there is a skunk close by!

PW

71

RECIPES FOR:

Seeing Red Sangria   NO Sex on the Beach

Repeat Pickled Shrimp

Beach Bum Shrimp   Hot N Crabby Cream Cheese Dip   Marinated Fruit Stash

Fishy Chicken Salad   Tiny Shark Bites/Dilly Dilly Sauce   Spicy Ripe Olives

Southern Boy Getcha Cookies   Moonin' Booty Bars   Pale Blonde Brownies

PW

FISHY GOURMET BEACH LUNCH

BEACH BUM SHRIMP
You need to boil 3 lb. medium Shrimp in: 4 to 5 Qt. Water   1 quartered onion   2 quartered lemons   2 T oil
3 halved celery stalks   3 T lemon juice   1 shrimp boil bag   1 tsp cayenne pepper
Boil for 20 minutes.....add Shrimp.....boil 3 to 4 minutes. Turn off heat and let sit for 3 to 4 minutes. Remove shrimp.
Add 12 to 15 whole lil new potatoes.....cook about 20 minutes. Add 8 small ears of corn after the potatoes have cooked
10 minutes. After cooking, remove from water, add shrimp to corn and potatoes. Serve with Chili Sauce .
DELICIOUS AND GUARANTEED TO SPICE UP YOUR LIFE AND HEAT UP BOB!!!

HOT 'N CRABBY CREAM CHEESE DIP
In a pretty baking dish, mix all the following together: 1 8 oz Cream cheese   1 C crab meat   2 T finely chopped onion
1 T milk $\frac{1}{2}$ tsp horseradish $\frac{1}{4}$ tsp salt   pepper to taste
Sprinkle with 1/3 C chopped almonds and bake at 375° for about 30 minutes. Serve with different colored vegetables.
THIS IS AS CRABBY AS SMELLY BOBBY BUT OH, SOOOOO DELICIOUS!

REPEAT PICKLED SHRIMP
YOU'D LIKE TO DO THIS TO MELBA, BUT SHE MIGHT TASTE TOOOO GOOD!
Place 5 lb. Shrimp, in their Shells, into a roasting pan with 1 lb butter.
Add: a 2 oz can of Black Pepper   juice of 4 lemons and a lg bottle Italian Dressin
Stir all together and cook, covered, for 45 minutes at 350°. Dump onto a lg platter, THEN PEEL'EM AND EAT'EM.
BETTER PUT A BIB ON BEACH-BUYIN' BOB!!!

MARINATED FRUIT STASH
Using the amount of fruit you need, place: orange sections   chunks of pineapple, canteloupe, honeydew melon, and
white/red seedless grapes in a bowl and set aside.
Boil together: 2/3 C orange juice, 3 T minced Ginger, 3 T honey. Cool. Add $\frac{1}{2}$ C Mayo, $\frac{1}{2}$ C Yogurt. Mix and Pour over fruit.

FISHY CHICKEN SALAD

Combine: a small pkg Albacore Tuna   1 ½ C diced pineapple chunks   Blend ¾ C Mayo, ¼ to ½ C Sour Cream,
2 C cubed, cooked Chicken   ¼ C shredded carrots   1 tsp curry powder, 1 tsp lemon juice,
1 ½ C diced celery   ½ C salted almond halves   ½ tsp salt with fishy, chicken mixture.
3 small finely chopped scallions with greens
SERVE WITH TOASTED, GARLIC MELBA ROUNDS

TINY SHARK BITES/DILLY DILLY SAUCE

Mix 1 lb chopped shark meat or catfish fillets with: ¾ C breadcrumbs   3 minced green onions   2 lg eggs   ½ tsp salt
½ C finely chopped Red Pepper   ¼ tsp cracked black pepper

Shape into 12 patties, dredge in breadcrumbs. Cook in hot oil for 3 to 4 minutes. Drain. Serve with following:
1 C Mayonnaise   2 C Sour Cream   2 T dried Dill Weed   1 T Parsley   dash of Salt.....ALL Mixed Together.....IT IS
AS DILLY, SILLY AS THINKIN' I WOULD HAVE COMPANY FOR MY BEACH LUNCH!!!

SPICY RIPE OLIVES

Drain 1 pt jar of pitted Ripe Olives (reserve liquid)....Add the following to the jarred olives:
1 small dried Chili Pepper   2 cloves crushed Garlic   ½ tsp dried dill   3 T Olive Oil Fill jar with reserved liquid.
Allow Olives to marinate for at least 2 days, LIKE YOU WANT TO DO TO MELBA.....BUT FOR A MONTH!!!!!

SOUTHERN BOY GETCHA COOKIES

Combine 1 pkg of store-bought Brownie Mix with ½ C Oil   ¼ C of prepared Instant Coffee (cold)   ¼ C Kahlua
Bake as the directions indicate.
YOU CAN SURE STAND BOB AND MELBA AFTER EATIN ONE OF THESE YUMMIES!

MOONIN' BOOTY BARS

Line a 9 X 13 pan with 1 C chopped Pecans. Bake at 350° for 4 to 5 minutes, stirring abit. Remove from pan.
Heavily grease the same pan and set aside. Stir together: 1 pkg dry yellow cake mix   2 ½ C uncooked Oats
and ¾ C melted Butter until mixture is moist and crumbly. Press half this mixture into the greased pan and top with the
toasted pecans and 1 12 oz pkg Milk Chocolate Morsels. Add remaining Oat mixture and Bake at 350 for about 30
minutes or until golden brown. Cut into desired bar sizes. Microwave and Melt 25 Caramels in 1 T water.....pour over bars.
            LAWDY! LAWDY! THESE ARE TOOOOO GOOD TO BE ASSOCIATED WITH A BOOTY!!!

PALE BLONDE BROWNIES

Combine: 2 C All-Purpose Flour   2 tsp Baking Powder
                       ½ C Butter   2 C packed Brown Sugar
                       2 Eggs   1 tsp Vanilla
                    1 C chopped Pecans or Walnuts

Grease a 9 X 13 pan and spread mixture into it. Bake at 350° for 20 to 25 minutes. Cut into square while warm.
            THIS'LL KNOCK 'OL BOB INTO A COMA.....IF YOU'RE LUCKY!!!

PW

GOLDILOCKS AND BAD, BAD, BOB

House parties are always so interesting, you never know what to expect, especially when your spouse is makin' eyes at the 'hostess with the mostest.' Ol' VooDoo Bob could charm your panties off with all the malarkey comin out of his lustful, lascivious, 'mouth from the South.' Don Juan looked like a pussycat compared to Roberto, The Romeo of West Tennessee!

At this particular party, I just stood back and watched Bob circling Susie Q like a buzzard waitin to swoop the booty, I mean bounty! Little Cutie Pie was just winkin' and blinkin' the night away in her, all gussied-up, yellow, strapless, skintight, too short mini dress with butterflies on her boobies. The libations were flowin'...Bob the Vulture was glowin', and suddenly, Mister Gotcha Prey was NO SHOWIN'.

The Host of the House, while entertaining the other guests, began searching for his Princess Butterfly, when in-a-flash, she appeared like magic! She was practically incandescent with enthusiasm or, as my old grandmother use to say, "She was Red-Hot!" Bad Bad Bob entered from the opposite direction looking like the 'Cat that ate the Canary. Did I mention precious Susie Q had long, yellow-blonde curls???

I floated ever so gracefully to the overflowing food table and stared, like a Zombie, at the most delicious Creations of Culinary Art. WOW...I was impressed...Goldilocks sure knew her STUFF and she could cook too!!!

TIP: My old Grandmother would also say, "Make sure your panties don't have holes, just in case you have a car wreck and have to go to the hospital." Or I might add....an encounter of any Sort or Size!!!

RECIPES FOR:

Hot-To-Trot Artichoke Squares   Ham 'n Cheese Rolls in the Hay   Balls of Spinach
Garlic 'n Big Sausage Stuffed Mushrooms   HURRY! HURRY! Curry Dip   Salami Horns of Plenty

GOLDILOCKS AND BAD, BAD, BOB   LC

HOT TO TROT ARTICHOKE SQUARES

2 (6 oz) jars marinated artichoke   1 mined onion   4 large eggs   1 (8 oz) package mozzarella cheese   ¼ C dried bread crumbs   2 T chopped parsley   ¼ t salt   ¼ t pepper. Drain liquid from 1 jr of artichoke into 1 quart saucepan. Chop all artichokes.   In liquid in saucepan, cook onion. Beat eggs. Stir in onion, artichokes, mozzarella cheese, bread crumbs, parsley, salt and pepper. Spread in greased 12 x 8 pan, bake 30 – 35 minutes at 325°. Cut into squares. BEAR HUG BOB LOVED GOLDIES HOT TO TROT SQUARES !

HAM 'N CHEESE ROLLS IN THE HAY

1 (8 oz) package cream cheese, softened   2 T prepared horseradish or ¼ C chopped green onions   1 package sliced, ham.   Combine cream cheese and horseradish or onions. Spread mixture on double ham slices; roll and secure with toothpick. Chill; slice rolls. HIGH ROLLER ROBERT STRIKES AGAIN !

BALLS OF SPINACH

1 (10 oz) package frozen spinach   2 beaten eggs   ½ C shredded cheddar cheese   ¼ C butter   1 (8.5 oz) package corn muffin mix   ½ C chopped onion   ½ C Parmesan cheese   ½ C bleu cheese dressing   1/8 t garlic powder. Cook spinach and onion as directed on package. Drain and press out all liquid. Combine all ingredients and mix well. Cover and chill for 2 hours. Shape into 1-inch balls and freeze. Bake at 350 ° for 10 – 12 minutes. BE BALLSY, BOBBY WAS !

GARLIC 'N BIG SAUSAGE STUFFED MUSHROOMS

1 (8 oz) package cream cheese softened   ½ C cooked crumbled sausage   1 T chopped green onion   ¼ t garlic powder   ½ C shredded cheddar cheese   1 lb whole fresh mushrooms, stems removed.   In small mixing bowl, beat cream cheese until smooth. Stir in bacon, onion and garlic powder. Spoon into mushroom caps. Place on ungreased broiler pan. Broil 4 -6 inches from the heat for 4-6 minutes or until heated through. Serve warm. STUFFED SAUSAGE IS ALWAYS A WINNER !

HURRY! HURRY! CURRY DIP

½ pint mayonnaise   2 T minced onion   dash of garlic salt   2 T curry powder   1 t lemon juice   3 T catsup   1 T Worcestershire sauce   dash of hot sauce. Mix all ingredients. Dip. HURRY, HURRY CATCH THE CURRY !

SALAMI HORNS OF PLENTY

1 lb. salami , sliced thin   1 container herbed- cream cheese.   Roll salami into cones and pipe cheese in with a pastry bag, or spread layer of cream cheese over salami and roll into cone shape. Secure with toothpicks if necessary. STICK THAT TOOTHPICK IN THE SALAMI!

LC

GOIN' TO THE RIVER DINNER

One lovely Spring evening, in the midst of internal turmoil and external anxiety, I had, like a Stepford wife, prepared a delicious meal for my two kiddies and their meandering father. Although, I NEVER knew if Captain Bob would make it to dinner or if there would be another meetin' down by the River!!! This Meetin' Thing was happening at least two or three nights a week.....for BUSINESS???

There was another meetin' alright, but ol Ballsey knew he had just about pushed that scenario to the limit. He figured he better make it for dinner and feel the situation out before talkin' about leavin' for another so-called meeting! After all, he had already encountered two 'River Conferences' this week.....Bob did not want to push his luck too far! So, he graced his family with his presence and put on a Show to-beat-none!

The Perfect Father brought in two playthings for each child, motorized of course, and they thought they were in Toy Heaven! How slick can you get? Encountering Bob even played with his surprised little children for about twenty minutes! Oh, what a night!!! This is One to put down on paper, date it, and take a picture! Excitedly, he sat down with his two grateful children and catchin-the-drift wife, filled his mouth with scrumptious food, and praised every morsel. Oh, Brother!

With an over-stuffed mouth I thought I heard Bob mumble something about a meeting...River....7:00. I kept smiling as though I never heard those dreaded words, and I thought to myself, "Excited alright...but not for the same reason baby girl and boy are. You just can't wait for THAT BUMPING, JUMPING, THRILLING RIVER RIDE!" For me, it was my Last Cruise on the Stream of Deceit!

A few bites of Lasagna were munched before I politely excused myself, and gathered my two happy toddlers for a little trip down the basement stairs to the backyard. Our anxiously awaiting Boxer, BoBo, was ready to play...he loved those motor-driven things too! AirBoatBob should have realized All Hell was about to break loose, but he kept on eatin'. Guess he figured he needed his strength down at the River! On my way up, I passed Simon, the Siamese Cat and noticed his hair was standing on end! You know they say Cats can tell when ARMAGEDDON IS COMING!!!!

PW

Bob's sweet and very busy wife had NOT been calm since the Record Shop incident….Hell, since the precious babies had been born! These children were suppose to keep her so busy, Good Wife wouldn't even remember there was a River!!! That's when HoudiniBob did his greatest disappearing acts. But she was a busy wife, but not too busy to pick up on Big Round MOONS Over The River…if you get the drift!!!

Bob just kept on choppin' and smiling, and the little perky wife and mother of two toddlers, three cats, one dog, five fish, eight gerbils, and two rabbits also kept on smiling and waiting for the perfect moment to put on HER act! Bob's energy gulping never ceased….I do believe his 'River Jolt' anticipation was getting the best of him!

Busy Wife slowly, Slow Burning that is, walked around to her side of the table, braced her shaky hands beneath, and unexpectedly FLIPPED that full table of food all over Bob's goin to the river, stylish blue-stripped suit!!! Suddenly, Lasagna became Upsidedown Insideout Ravioli. The two vegetable dishes became Tossed Hodgepodge Salad. Warm Apricot Apple Cake became Apple Pastry Smothered in Sauce. The Bread, well, the sticky, buttery Garlic Delight ended up on Bob's head…..and my beautiful garnet Cabernet gave new meaning to the word Designer!!! Damn I hated loosing that wine!

TIP: Whenever you anticipate a River Thing, don't feed your animals all day. Just open the door and
      Let Them Feast! Be Careful…..Use Plastic Dinnerware.

RECIPES FOR:

    Upsidedown Insideout Ravioli   Tossed Hodgepodge Salad
              Dirty Garlic Bread
       Warm Apple Cake Smothered in Apricot Sauce
     Ready To Drink Iced Tea   A great Cabernet Sauvignon

PW

GOIN TO THE RIVER DINNER

UPSIDEDOWN INSIDEOUT RAVIOLI
Brown 1 ½ lb lean Ground Beef with 1 lg chopped Onion
    And 1 clove Garlic.
Add: 1 8 oz jar mushrooms   1 8 oz can Tomato Sauce
Bits.

        1 6 oz can Tomato Paste   1 tsp salt/pepper
                    1 tsp sugar
Cook 1 10 oz pkg chopped frozen Spinach as directed.
Drain off the spinach liquid in a measuring cup, then add
enough water to make 1 C.   Add liquid to meat mixture.
Meantime, cook 1 8 oz pkg Shell Macaroni.
For the Filling, Mix together:
        1 8 oz shredded Cheddar Cheese
        1 8 oz shredded Mozzarella Cheese
        2 beaten Eggs
        ¼ C Salad Oil
        drained Spinach
        ½ C Breadcrumbs
        Cooked Shell Macaroni
In a 9X13 Baking pan, layer half the Filling...top with Meat
Sauce, then the rest of Filling.....top with 1 C Parmesan Cheese.
Bake at 350° for 25 minutes.
TOO DELICIOUS TO END UP ON TOP BOB!!!

PW

TOSSED HODGEPODGE SALAD
Dump a pkg of Spring Mix Lettuce Greens
into a bowl with thinly sliced cucumbers,
cherry tomato halves, and ½ pkg Real Bacon

Mix with the following **LUSCIOUS HOMEMADE DRESSIN:**
    Combine all....blend well.....chill
    1 pt Real Mayonnaise
    1 pt Buttermilk
    Juice of ½ Lemon
    1 pkg Garlic Salad Dressing Mix
    1 pkg Italian Salad Dressing Mix
    1 pkg Green Onion Salad Dressing Mix
    1/2 tsp Sugar
    ½ tsp Salt
LOVE IT.....SO DO THE KIDS AND THE PETS.

GARLIC GREEN BEANS
Drain a can of tiny green beans...rinse.
Saute beans in: 1 T butter   1 T Olive Oil
3 Garlic cloves   1 tsp salt/pepper
                DELIGHTFUL!

DIRTY GARLIC BREAD

Slice a whole loaf of Italian bread.....lengthwise.
Cut in slices to within 1 inch of bottom.
Heat: ½ C butter...1 clove garlic...1 T Italian Seasoning
Pour over top and sides of bread.
Bake at 275° for 25 minutes.
EXCELLENT FOR EATIN AND STAININ'!!!

WARM APPLE CAKE

For a wonderful MOIST Cake, combine ALL the list,
pour into a greased and floured 9 X 13 pan, and Bake
at 350 for about 40 minutes:

½ C butter	2 eggs
1 C sugar	1 C Sugar Substitute
2 C all-purpose flour	1 tsp salt
1 tsp cinnamon	1 tsp vanilla
1 tsp baking soda	½ C raisins
1 C walnuts or pecans	4 C diced apples

SMOTHER IN THE FOLLOWING:

APRICOT SAUCE

For 20 minutes, rapidly cook 1 lg can apricots with juice
and ½ C sugar.....remove from heat and sieve if desired.
Pour over warm cake...great over sponge cake or ice cream.
PW

READY TO DRINK OR TOSS ICED TEA

Combine the following:
3 qt medium-strength Tea
½ C sugar
1 12 oz can frozen lemonade
concentrate
Just before serving, stir in 1 qt COLD
Ginger Ale. Pour over glasses of
crushed ice and thin slices of lemon.

THIS IS GUARANTEED TO COOL YOU
DOWN AFTER A GOOD TABLE TOSSIN'.

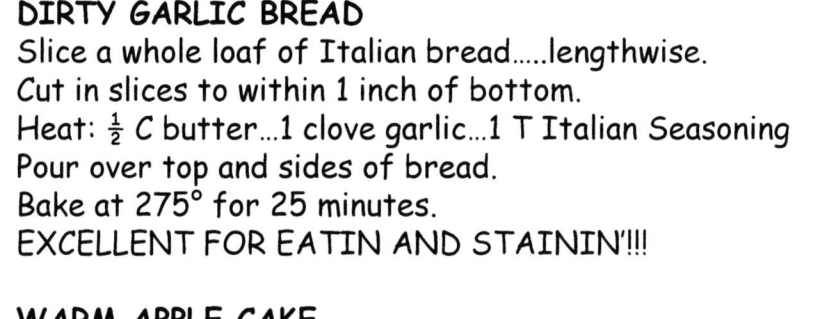

HIGH-HEELED MOLLY

I AM LEAVIN'. I AM WALKING OUT THAT DOOR NOW you Cheatin Jackass!!!!! DO YOU HEAR ME? Big-eared Bob could hear alright, but listening was definitely NOT one of his greatest assets. He wasn't responding, but he was thinking. If Molly walked out on him it would make All the Suspicious Rumors RIGHT.....Bob couldn't have that! He had a business and clients that thought he hung the moon.

Furthermore, everybody thought his family was so cute, and look at all that Molly did for the community! Bob cared for Molly down deep, WAY DOWN DEEP, down so far he could hardly muster a feelin. But, Bob needed someone to listen to his Bologna, to play football with him, to mama the kids, to fix his dinner, and to take care of the animals HE JUST HAD TO HAVE!!!!! But, you know, the man never even called those pets by their right names! Sometimes he called 'em Jack and Ginger, and Jack was BoBo, and Ginger was Mama Kitty, or Simon was Molly!!! No matter, Bob needed to take some quick, smart action by damn.. "She is not gonna walk out that door," Sinister, Beady-eyed Bob thought!

Now you see, Molly was of a short statue so she wore fancy high heel shoes ALL THE TIME! She wore them with everything and everywhere she went, even to the market. She musta had 80 to 100 pairs, maybe more! Molly was 'somebody' when she donned those tiny feet. She loved those high heels cause they made her feel good when she wore em', a whole lot better than Bad Bob made her feel! Distressed, Molly click-clacked out the front door to walk the neighborhood and gather her thoughts.

Easy Chair Conniving Bob jumped up, knowing it would take her an extra long time in those heels. He eased his way to the basement, embracing the aroma of the wonderful dinner Molly had earlier prepared. He grabbed a hammer and a block of wood and ran to Molly's closet. He came face-to-face with the high heel weapons that had almost stuck in his rear a time or two in the past. Carpenter Bob proceeded to dismantle the artillery of every color and every make by knocking the heels off every single pair!!!!!

He climbed back upstairs, then placed the splintered esteem-builders all back on their racks or in their boxes and said with a devious laugh, "Guess you won't be walking anywhere ol Molly Girl." He then gathered ALL those knocked-off spikes, slithered back to the basement, smelled that great aroma again, then deposited every last one of 'em in his golf bag. He was thinking about the Lake where the teenagers often gathered after midnight. Bob's thoughts were more sinister than ever…."Next time some goofball goes diving for golf balls, he'll be pullin' up high heel spikes and thinking…What The Hell….that'll get 'em!"

As puffed up as an old adder, Bob took himself to the kitchen and quickly filled his plate and his stomach. He had really worked up an appetite just thinking up this scheme, much less running up and down the stairs!!! Bob was also thinking this really just might be his LAST DINNER!

TIP: Don't ever Heel-Pop unless dinner is ready and waiting!
     Next time, don't SAY you're walkin' out, JUST DO IT, and don't be wearing any high heel shoes!!!

RECIPES FOR:

Grilled Bob-O-Qued Bologna Cubes   HoneyDidDew Coolers

Devious Deviled Eggs and Stacked Lettuce Salad with Hammered Blue Cheese Dressing

Molly's Broiled Short Ribs   Pump 'n Dumplins   Knock-Your-Heels-Off Tomatoes with Peas

Way Down Deep Peach Cobbler

PW

HIGH-HEELED MOLLY

GRILLED BOB-O-QUED BOLOGNA CUBES

Buy ya a big hunk Bologna round...cut 1 inch slices.
Marinade in your favorite BBQ sauce for about
1 hour. Grill, watchin carefully cause it will burn up!
When beautiful and dark brown, take from heat and
Cut into cubes..."IN THE SOUTH THIS IS LIKE
EATIN A STEAK...DELICIOUS!" CLAIMS BOB."

STACKED LETTUCE SALAD

In a pretty lil salad bowl tear 1 small lettuce head
Into bite-sized pieces. Sprinkle 3 grated radishes on top.
Layer the following on top the radish:
    1 thinly sliced cucumber   ½ pt halved cherry tomatoes
    ½ C lil cauliflower pieces   4 oz alfalfa sprouts
4 cooked/crumbled bacon slices   1 C whole wheat croutons
Top with Homemade Blue Cheese Dressin

DEVIOUS DEVILED EGGS

Boil 1 doz eggs and slice lengthwise. Remove
yolks and mix them with:
    6 T mayonnaise   ¾ T chopped pickled jalapenos
    1 T mustard   ½ tsp cumin   1/8 tsp salt
        Fill the egg halves.....top with cilantro

HAMMERED BLUE CHEESE DRESSING

Blend the following until smooth:
1 8 oz container whipped herb/garlic cream cheese
    ½ C Buttermilk
    ¼ C chopped green onions with tops
    1 tsp lemon juice
    ¼ C Real mayonnaise
    a dash of salt/pepper
        Mix in 4 oz crumbled Blue Cheese. Cover/Chill

MOLLY'S BROILED SHORT RIBS

Sprinkle 4 lb beef short ribs with salt/pepper.....cut into small serving pieces.....Place in a Dutch oven adding water
to cover.....Simmer covered about 2 hours or until tender.....Drain pieces and place on a rack of a broiler pan.....
Combine: 2/3 C Catsup   ¼ C light Molasses   ¼ C Lemon juice   1 T Mustard   ½ tsp Chili powder
        Several dashes Garlic powder   Brush over ribs and continue bastin' while they are broiling 4 to 5 inches
        from the heat for about 10 to 15 minutes. YOU'RE GONNA LOVE EM!
PW

PUMP 'N DUMPLINS
Combine the following:
   1 C flour   ½ tsp baking powder   ½ tsp salt
   1 egg   ½ C milk or more if needed when mixin
   ¼ C Canola oil   Stir til combined.....Drop by
   spoonfuls into hot, bubbly chicken broth. Cover.
   Reduce heat and simmer 12 to 15 minutes.
GOOD!

KNOCK-YOUR-HEELS-OFF TOMATOES WITH PEAS
   Purchase round, good-tastin tomatoes. Slice how
   many you need in half. Scoop out the pulp and fill
   cups with tiny green peas. Place on a broiler and
   sprinkle with garlic/parsley salt. Place a T butter
   on top each. Watchin carefully, run through the
   Broiler for just a few minutes. SO CUTE AND
   GOOD!

WAY DOWN DEEP PEACH COBBLER
Mix together and set aside:
   3 C sliced fresh peaches   1/3 C granulated Sugar   ¼ C Brown sugar   a good dash of both nutmeg/cinnamon
   Melt 1 stick butter in a 9 X 13 baking pan   Stir: ½ C granulated   ¾ C flour   2 tsp bakin' powder together
   to make a batter.....Pour this over the melted butter...not stirring. Next, spoon the Peach mixture over the batter.
Bake at 350° for 45 minutes. Serve warm with ice cream.   A REALLY LUSCIOUS TREAT!

PW

HOOK, LINE, AND SINK HER

Trips to the lake for sailin' and skiin' were usually so much fun, even though YOU had to pack everything including the kitchen sink! Hopefully you'd have time to make yourself look a little sexy as well! Things were always tense with Bobby and myself, particularly with rumors around town of his infidelities. Every divorcee client was bait and even good friends were questionable. So, like a Dummy, I kept thinking, looking good had something to do with stayin' together!!! At the lake, little Jack and precious Ginger had their Daddy and his full attention, or so I thought anyway. This trip, two good friend families went to share in the fun and food. For awhile I could leave thoughts of the infidel BoBob behind and take along Robert, the father and husband. Sounded good anyway!!!

Yummy cookout meals were planned, ingredients bought, and we were off to the Lake! Jack and Ginger were a bit fussy, each wanting what the other had, kinda like their Daddy was about all our friend's wives. But as we met with Jay, JenniBeth, their two boys and the other family, grouchiness turned to playfulness. All was well! Too well as I took a look at JenniBeths skimpy water wear! Plus, her 'long ass' brown hair kept floating in the breeze tangling in WayTooFriendlyBobs face. Strange enough, he always managed to NEED whatever just happened to be next to her slightly pudgy body. "Bob is SUCH a good husband…so HELPFUL…how on earth would you manage without him," JenniBeth laughingly said. Funny, I had been thinking that same thing A WHOLE LOT lately!

We water-skied, we floated on large inner tubes, we laughed, we played cards, we drank frosty coolers while Bob and JenniBeth prepared the grills and tables for our luscious lakeside feast. She was one of those DoGooder people who just HAD to DO everything! While they kept busy, I could see that MUCH conversation ensued between the two Flirtatious Flits. But suddenly, as quick as a wind, AnxiousBob came bouncing into the water, announcing he and I had just enough time for one last spin around the lake before the cooking aromas filled the campsite. I turned to Jack and Gin who were once again fussing-the-day-away and asked Bea and Rog to keep a close-eye on my battling babes. I wasn't sure I wanted to take that short escape….Heaven Help Me!

I watched JenniBeth's cunning stare as I boarded the ski boat. Apprehension gripped my being but I happily waved to the two splashing siblings. As we circled the lake taking in the rays and warm water breeze, Bob kept insisting I don my ski. "Just show em what you can do," he encouragingly shouted. If I had my wits about me, I would have realized this was some kind of game…..Bob NEVER complemented me! But I had just enough baking-of-the-brain from sun and coolers…YES, I would show that witch-haired siren just how good I could ski! You know, of course, JenniBeth was good at EVERYTHING!!!!

Bob stopped, I jumped in but he didn't drop my favorite ski. Nor had I put on my precious-to-life ski vest!! YEK! I knew my predicament and so did my Mean-to-the-Bone husband. "HELP ME BOB, HELP ME," I gargled. Instead, he took off in a circle around me making huge waves and laughing insidiously. I bobbed up and down like a fisherman's cast gulping air and dark water. Lights-of-my-life flashed before me. I WAS GOIN UNDER!!!!! I could see and hear the motor comin close. I mustered all within me to reach the sunlight, thinking of nothing but Jack and Ginger.

Well, I do believe my babies' irritability saved the day!!! I kept reaching for Bob's arm that apparently wasn't leavin' his side...I saw an evil grin come over his devilish face as he kept glancing toward the shore. Thank God Jack and Gin were still at it, screamin' and splashin' like baby water moccasins. I literally felt Bob's thoughts.....he might as well have spoken them.....second thoughts on raising two youngin's without their Mama!! In an instant Bob's manliness turned to a limp noodle....Thank you Jesus for that and for sending Angels to my rescue....Angels that weren't scared of a MeanAss husband!!!

I made it back to my babies. I made it back to cook the luscious tenderloin and cherish every morsel. I made it back with a new and troublesome fear! But, I kept smiling...didn't have much choice for the moment. Just to hear my two children screaming was delightful!!!

TIP: Never go on a boat with ANY Bob without a Life Vest!
　　　You know, your 'LOOKS' have nothing to do with a cheatin Husband...OK??? Look good for YOURSELF!

RECIPES FOR:

　　　　　To Die For Melon Coolers　　　　　　Flirtatious Flitinis　　　　　　DoGooder Limeade

　　　MeanAss Deviled Eggs　　　Limp Noodle Lakeside Salad　　　Honey Drippin Sesame Chicken Bites
Screamin Pimento Cheese Spread　　　Whole Wheat Crackers　　　Help Me! Help Me! Salmon Cream Cheese Olive Spread

　　　Almost Roasted Corn-on-the-Cob　　　Insidious Grilled Pork Tenderloin on Whole Wheat Buns
　　　　　JBs Cunning Grilled Veggie Medley　　　　　Second Thoughts Toasted Garlic Bread

　　　Splashin' Siblings Strawberry Homemade Ice Cream　　　　Sinsational Devils Food Cake

　　　　　　　　　　　　　　　　　　　　　　　　　　　　　　　　　　PW

HOOK, LINE, AND SINK HER

MEANASS DEVILED EGGS
Mix All the following with the yolks of 1 doz boiled eggs:
   2 T mayonnaise   1 T mustard   1 T sweet relish
   ½ tsp sugar   ½ tsp vinegar   dash pepper/salt
            2 dashes garlic/parsley salt
Fill the egg halves with the mixture...sprinkle with paprika

SCREAMIN PIMENTO CHEESE SPREAD
Mix all together and refrigerate this SPICY dish:
1 ¼ C mayonnaise   12 oz jar chopped roasted Red peppers
1 T grated onion   1 tsp powdered mustard   dash of garlic salt
dash black pepper   1 tsp lemon juice   2 10 oz shredded
      SO TASTY!   Colby-Jack cheese

HELP ME! HELP ME!
SALMON CREAM CHEESE OLIVE SPREAD
Mix All the following....shape into a ball....roll in chives:
1 8 oz vegetable/herb cream cheese   ½ C chopped stuffed green olives
3 T mayonnaise   a splash of Honey-Mustard dressin   ½ C chopped pecans
1 large package of crumbled Pink Salmon GREAT ON WHOLE WHEAT CRACKERS
                        OR CRUSTY BREAD ROUNDS.

PW

SESAME CHICKEN BITES
Cook a lg bag skinless chicken fillets.
Cut into bite-sized pieces. Mix the
following for a batter:
   2 beaten eggs   3 oz sesame seeds
   1 C water   1 ½ tsp salt   1 C flour
      Dip chicken and Fry

LIMP NOODLE LAKESIDE SALAD
To a prepared 12 oz pkg of Penne pasta,
 add; 1 6 oz crumbled Feta cheese
            1 4 oz diced/drained pimentos
            1 small bottle green olives
         1 small can sliced black olives
         1 bunch chopped green onions
         half C small broccoli florets
         1 small bag cooked salad shrimp
Mix all together with bottled Greek dressin

INSIDIOUS GRILLED PORK TENDERLOIN

Rub a 2 to 3 lb pork tenderloin with the following: 1 tsp garlic powder   1 tsp salt   1 tsp dry mustard   ½ tsp pepper

Lots of chopped Rosemary and Basil

Lightly spray with cooking oil   Grill, covered, about 12 minutes on each side over a medium flame

Remove from grill and let stand about 10 minutes then slice or chop for a DELICIOUS sandwich:

Drizzle the meat with a light onion barbeque sauce...place on whole wheat buns with Arugula lettuce/thin slice tomato

JB'S CUNNING GRILLED VEGGIE MEDLEY

Prepare the following vegetables in ¼inch lengthwise cuts:

1 medium (skin on) Eggplant   2 yellow Squash   2 Zucchini

3 Vadalia Onions   1 yellow Bell pepper/1 red Bell pepper

Grill over medium heat for 3 to 5 minutes on each side.

Toss the hot veggies with a prepared or homemade Pesto.

ALMOST ROASTED CORN-ON-THE-COB

Buy 6 to 8 ears of corn.....shuck/silk removed
Cut in half and place them on a sheet of foil each
Top with lots of butter.....garlic powder.....
sprinkles of a salad supreme mix.....sprinkle
of salt/pepper.....Wrap tight to seal but loose
around the corn.....Grill on top rack until tender
(20 to 30 min)..... turn a few times.

SINSATIONAL DEVILS FOOD CAKE

Prepare a devil food cake mix as directions indicate and bake in a rectangular pan

and ice with the following SINFUL Icing: Bring just to a boil...3 T cocoa   6 T milk   1 stick butter

Remove from heat and add 1 box sifted powdered sugar   2 tsp vanilla   1 C chopped pecans

Pour this over the cake while BOTH are hot.....OUT OF THIS WORLD JUST LIKE BOB!!!

SPLASHIN' SIBLINGS STRAWBERRY HOMEMADE ICE CREAM

Mix together: 1 qt mashed fresh strawberries   1 ½ C sugar   2 13 oz evaporated milk   1 T lemon juice

Refrigerate until well chilled then pour into a 2 qt ice cream freezer container. Churn and Freeze. OH MY!!!

DOGOODER LIMEADE To a large frozen limeade mix...add: ½ Gallon Lime Sherbet...2 cans cold lemon/lime soda /Blend

PW

HOTEL, MOTEL, NO TELL

Doctor Ima Butcher was a tall, slender, brunette, female Surgeon in Bob's Practice. Bobby considered Butchy to be his protégé and was determined to guide her caREAR and anything else he could get his skuzzy hands on. Little did I know the Good Doctors were working after hours many a night at the Stardust Inn, until the fickle-finger-of-fate pointed the way!

MedicineMan Bob and his co-hart were spotted at an out-of-the-way Gourmet Market buying all sorts of Goodies. The Stardust advertised kitchenettes in every Cabin......WOWEE!!! How nice and charmingly convenient for the sorry, no-good JackASS Doctors.

 Doctors Bob and ImaSlut made their way to The Love Nest Inn in separate cars. Romantic Bob registered at the desk and asked for a secluded cabin near the River with a view. WHAT A MISTAKE! My forces were already on alert behind enemy lines. Ima showed up momentarily and hid her Sporty little car in a grove of trees overflowin' with, none-the-less...Poison Ivy Vines. God Is GOOD! You see, The Good Doctor Bob was highly allergic to the Ivy!

A little after Sunset, wonderful, delicious aromas of freshly baked Pizza floated through the evening air. I could faintly hear the POP of the Champagne. Round Two comin UP if Bob had remembered his Manly Pills! He always thought he was 'hung like a Bull'......I just thought he needed to be HUNG! I wanted to rush in and tell them to PUT A CORK IN IT!!! But Good Old Mother Nature, and the 'winding vine of revenge,' performed at will. Not only were the Pizza aromas filling the air, but so were the potent fumes of the poison ivy......Doctor beware!!!

Dr. FeelGood Bob graced the old home place just as the clock chimed midnight...the witching hour. He was looking rough around the edges. I immediately developed a hacking cough when Bob walked into the bedroom, quickly excused myself, and fled to the den couch......where I slept for the next TWO YEARS!!!

Calamine lotion, baking soda, itch medicine, and everything else I had in the medicine cabinet for UNFAITHFUL, DISHONEST, ADULTEROUS HUSBANDS, had mysteriously vanished from sight. Bob stayed under the shower half the night moaning like a whooped Pussycat. When he finally appeared he looked like a splotchy, red, limp noodle, which of course, is exactly what he always was!

LC

TIP: IF you cant stand the heat.....stay out of the kitchen!

RECIPES FOR:

Play Doctor Cheesy Pizza   In the Sack Mushroom Pizza   Mess around Meaty Pizza

LC

HOTEL MOTEL NO TELL

PLAY DOCTOR CHEESY PIZZA

1 prepared pizza crust   1 lb ground beef   1 pkg. taco seasoning mix   1 C salsa   1 pkg cheddar cheese shredded 1 bag tortilla chips. Brown ground beef with taco seasoning mix as directed on package. Spread beef over crust. Sprinkle cheese over ground beef. Bake 8 – 1- minutes at 450°. Remove from oven. Spread salsa over beef and cheese and sprinkle crushed tortilla chips over all. BED-SIDE MANNER BOB AND IMA BUTCHER WERE CHEESY EXPERTS !

IN THE SACK MUSHROOM PIZZA

Portabello mushroom caps   pizza sauce   cooked ground sausage   mozzarella cheese   chopped onion. Scrape out gills from mushroom caps. In the mushroom cap add pizza sauce and meat.   Sprinkle with cheese and onion. Bake at 400 ° until bubbly and browned. MUSHROOMS FOR MUSH-HEADS !

MESS AROUND MEATY PIZZA

6 English muffins, split   1 small can tomato paste   2 T sugar   1 t salt   2 T Worcestershire sauce   2 cloves garlic, diced   4 oz Mozzarella cheese, grated   ½ lb cooked sausage   oregano. Mix tomato paste, sugar, salt, Worcestershire sauce and garlic. Spread thinly on muffins. Sprinkle cheese over tomato mixture. Top with sausage. Sprinkle with oregano. Bake at 450 ° for 15 minutes. Food for the soul, if they had one!

LC

HUSBAND-IN-LAW

With divorce comes dating! After only a few rounds of this new sport I came to realize, ALL MALES ARE BOB'S!!! They're just different colors, sizes, and shapes. No matter how good they are, in some form or another, THEY'RE ALL BOB'S!

Well, after divorcing the Baddest Bob in any town around the world, I tried to find a Bob of much lesser degree. Jack, Ginger, and I married an older, not much wiser, Italian gentleman, MarioRoberto. This Roberto loved, I mean really LOVED not only to EAT, but to COOK. He also LOVED to drink his Vino and was therefore, a very jolly Mario! I began to know we were in trouble when one day he said, "You know, I really like that ol fool Bob."

Jack and Ginger's Bobino, who came to visit on occasion, was in regard of our new Bob and respectfully referred to Mario as his Husband-In-Law! One such visit, Bob invited the four of us to dinner at a very impressive Four Star Restaurant. Upon arriving at this much-desired eatery, Bob immediately ordered his usual Rum 'n Coke and filled our ears with his bizarre client absurdities. All the while, MarioRoberto filled RummyBobs wine glass with the reddest and strongest Vino Italy had to offer. BobinoBob was always full-of-himself, but was now full of his Rum and Marios Wine! His eyes were quickly becoming as glazed as the spectacular peach sauce over the Brie appetizer! More food, Wine, and Rum were ordered than were on the menu! I thought to myself…"fantastic…spend all your money ol Bobino, cause you sure never did it when we were married!!!"

Our merriment continued as 'stuttering Bob' announced, "I gotta go pee." You could hear those large white Oxfords clomp away from the table and you could see him bouncing off the expensive walls of the restaurant. We continued to eat our delicious four course dinner and thanked God for the peace of Silence. Time passed, no Bob. We continued to eat and thank God, but still there was no Bob! After we downed our luscious desserts and wiped our mouths with rich, white linens….. still, no Bob! The very expensive check arrived, and, but of course, there was no Bobino!!!

The Husband-In-Law did the honors. We boxed Bob's meal, checked the restrooms and the other tables, but still no Bob. I sighed and cursed like a bedeviled she-dog inside but laughed on the outside. I apologized to our new and bewildered MarioRoberto and to my children. The three of us were NOT muddled…..WE KNEW from experience Bobino was close-by!!!

We left the restaurant with a lot less money and no Bob. As we turned the corner and headed into the parking area, we saw large, white Oxfords sticking out the back window of our car! THERE WAS BOB, out-like-a -light and in LaLa Land!!! He had put his drunken-self comfortably to bed in the backseat of our car!!! We, overstuffed-four, packed ourselves into the front seat like sardines, with Bob's boxed meal and headed home. I was convinced Bob had finally 'gone bananas'!!!

Lucky Jack had a tossing and turning Bobino-bed-partner that eventful night. The next morning Bob completely ignored the issue, maybe not even remembering a single thing!!! He just laughed, continued with his crazy tales, and ate his boxed dinner for breakfast. Proudly, he took home his Husband-In-Law's Italian leftovers from the week. You would have thought he had hit a jackpot! He and MarioRoberto hugged and shook hands for ten minutes....and I might add, that's the only one Bob embraced as he bide us goodbye!!!

Wow, we just couldn't wait for another Bob-Visit and invitation to dinner!

TIP: Next time Bob calls for another infamous dinner, GO OUT OF TOWN!
      If he catches you by surprise.....suggest a famous Fast Food....it's cheap and there's a Resident Clown
      just like Bob!!!

RECIPES FOR:

RummyBob Cocktails   Brie with Glazed-Over Peach Sauce
THEY'RE ALL BOB'S Brushetta   Stuffed Drunken-Self Lobster Tail
Husband-in-Law Spaghetti and Meatballs   Bedeviled She-Dog Crab
Drunken Spinach   Crackpot Jackpot Ginger/Sesame Rice
Tossin' 'n Turnin' Wilted Spinach Salad
LaLa Land Double Chocolate Cheesecake   Out-Like-A-Light Burgundy Pie

PW

HUSBAND-IN-LAW   PW

BRIE WITH GLAZED-OVER PEACH SAUCE
Trim/discard the top rind of an 8 oz Brie round.....place it in an oven-proof servin dish.....Top with ¼ C Peach Chutney
Bake at 400° for 10 minutes.....Sprinkle with chopped almonds.....Delicious with crackers or lil' bread rounds

THEY'RE ALL BOB'S BRUSHETTA
Cut a long Baguette bread into small rounds.....brush with an olive oil mixture of: 3 T olive oil   1 minced garlic clove
Toast at 350 for 12 minutes, depending on thickness, cool   Top with the following mixture: 2 finely chopped Avocados
2 diced plum tomatoes   2 chopped green onions   2 T lime juice   1 T wine vinegar
1 T olive oil   2 Tsp Hot sauce   ½ tsp garlic salt   Sprinkle with ¼ C chopped cilantro

WILTED SPINACH SALAD
Place 8 C torn Spinach in a bowl and add ¼ C sliced green onion   Sprinkle with lots of black pepper
Before cookin', cut 3 slices into small pieces.....Fry.....do not discard drippings.....Stir 1 T wine vinegar into Fry pan with
2 tsp lemon juice   ¼ tsp salt   ½ tsp sugar.....Remove from heat and stir in Spinach and green onions.....Gently coat.....
Top with 1 chopped hard-boiled egg.....Serve immediately   RUMMYBOB'S FAVORITE SO I DON'T SERVE IT OFTEN!

BEDEVILED SHE-DOG CRAB
Mix all the following together and bake at 350°, uncovered, for about 30 minutes:
1 cored chopped green pepper   1 C chopped celery   1 5 oz bag medium shrimp   1 6 oz can drained crabmeat
1 tsp Worcestershire sauce   1/8 tsp pepper   1 chopped onion   1 C mayonnaise   ½ tsp salt
Top with ½ C buttered bread crumbs

DRUNKEN-SELF LOBSTER TAIL
Cook 4 pkgs frozen Lobster tail.....cool and chop into bite-sized pieces.....Mix the following Sauce/Simmer/Smother
Lobster: ¼ C butter   ¼ C flour   1 ½ cream   ¼ C tomato paste   1 tsp garlic salt   1 t curry   ¼ t ginger   2 drops hot sauce
1 t lemon

CRACKPOT JACKPOT GINGER/SESAME RICE

Saute 1 C uncooked long grain rice in 2 T butter.....Stir in 1 tsp sesame seed   2 C chicken broth   ½ tsp salt pepper
½ tsp ginger   1 tsp lime juice   ¼ C chopped walnuts
Cover and cook for 25 minutes until rice is fluffy.....Serve with Lobster   SCRUMPTIOUS!

DRUNKEN SPINACH

Cook ½ lb chopped Italian sausage.....Drain.....Add: 3 beaten eggs   1 10 oz chopped drained Spinach   ¼ tsp salt/pepper
1 tsp garlic powder   ¼ C cottage cheese   2 C shredded Swiss cheese
Stir well then pour into a 9 inch unbaked pie crust.....Bake at 375° for 45 minutes or until golden brown
EVEN BOB'S KIDS WILL LOVE THIS SPINACH!

HUSBAND-IN-LAW SPAGHETTI AND MEATBALLS

Combine in a bowl: 1 ½ ground round   1 T onion   1 tsp cumin   1 tsp salt.....mix well and shape into 1 ½ balls
Brown in a skillet and set aside.....
In a large pot, cook 1 lb ground chuck, crumbling as you brown.....when thoroughly cooked.....Drain the fat then add:
1 chopped onion   1 C chopped celery   2 cloves chopped garlic   1 15 oz can tomato sauce   1 6 oz tomato paste
1 cup water   1 4 oz can mushroom pieces   2 tsp Oregano   1 tsp Italian seasoning mix   salt/pepper
Plop your little meatball into the sauce.....Bring to a boil then reduce heat and simmer about 1 ½ hours
May need to add water as it cooks
Cook your favorite pasta.....of course BOB'S FAVORITE IS THE GOOD OL LONG, STRAIGHT NOODLE!
MANGIARE ROBERTO! DIVERTIRSI!

OUT-LIKE-A-LIGHT BURGUNDY PIE

Stirring constantly, boil together: 5 C raspberries   1 C sugar   1 C Burgundy Wine
1 tsp grated lemon rind   3 T cornstarch
Reduce/cook 1 more minute, stirring.....pour into a baked 9 inch pie crust......thoroughly Chill.....Serve with whipped cream
GOOD JOB MARIOROBERTO!

PW

LALA LAND DOUBLE CHOCOLATE CHEESECAKE

Press 1 ½ C chocolate cream filled cookie crumbs (18 to 20 cookies) into the bottom of a 9 inch Spring-form pan

Melt down 1 12 oz pkg semisweet chocolate morsels.....add:

3 8 oz softened cream cheese   1 14 oz can sweetened milk   2 tsp vanilla   4 lg eggs

Blend well then pour into cookie crumb pan.....Bake at 300° for just a few minutes over an hour

Cool in the pan until the cake is at room temperature.....Cover and Chill about 8 hours.....Remove the sides

of the pan.....place on cake plate then drizzle chocolate syrup in little line up and down, runnin down the sides

of this ABSOLUTELY FANTASTIC CHOCOLATE FANTASY THAT BOB IS NOT IN!

PW

LEFTOVER DINNER

KNOCK! KNOCK! POUND! POUND! POUND! "What in Tarnation is goin on?" I said to myself. Ginger and Jack rushed to my bedside whispering, "Someone is at ouwa douwah!" I crept down the steps, peeked through the 'magic hole' and there stood two of my friends with their four kidos. Hugs and squeals of delight rang through the dark room. Although delighted to see them, I guess, this visit was certainly out of the ordinary!

Jody and Meg quickly announced, " you'll need to get your jackets and shoes on and come with us." They kept whispering that there was something I NEEDED to see! Now what did I NEED to see at this hour other than ZZZZZZ's or fluffy, ugly black sheep wooing me back to the nightmares of late! Well, I guess we would see, cause Jack and Gin were now full of anticipation of a new kind of play-night, and suspense was wrapping itself around my brain!

Off we went the same way they had come to my house...up the highway back toward the Lake where they had been eatin greasy but luscious fried Catfish and the best Hushpuppies and Slaw this side of the Mississippi River. The three adults, although I was beginning to doubt the maturity, piled into the front seat for a little 'quiet talk.' Our precious cargo filled the back section of the long station wagon. Meg proceeded to inform me they had seen ol BobbyBoy pass them on the highway, and following close behind was my good, Bestest FRIEND Ever, JenniBeth!

 All my friends and even Jenn's husband, Jay had tried, time after time, to convince me of B and J's illicit affair. But NO WAY!!!! NO FRIEND WOULD EVER DO THAT TO THEIR BESTEST FRIEND EVER!!!!!! After Jay's mysterious plane crash, CautiousBob had convinced me we should put an end to the gossip by cordially being seen out in public together with JenniBeth. "We should go to the Club for lunch and dinner soon," said my empathetic Bob. "This gesture will also help her to heal that whole tragic thing." But what was funny about that 'whole tragic thing', I thought to myself....I never once saw JenniBeth shed a tear, not one!!!

What appeared as an innocent drive from the Lake, turned out to be a Godsend! Upon actually seeing this supposed, fictitious romance actually take on a Life, Meg and Jody turned their car around and intriguingly followed the scoundrels. TricksterBob parked his car behind the Baptist Church of all places, and the Peachy Sweet Jenn whipped in quickly, picked him up, and the deceiving Snakes-In-The-Grass slithered their way up her driveway a coupla miles down the road. Thank you God for food cravin' in the dead of the night!!! Meg and Jody were my lifesavers! If Jody hadn't been 'with child' and craving those fried dill pickles, I'da been a true dumb blonde a whole lot longer! They had witnessed what had been suspected by many, for a long time!!!

After observing the evidence myself, I wrote out a note and stuck it under the slippery fishes windshield wiper. It simply said, "Now tell me it isn't so. See ya in the morning!!"
Brother, had I been taken down the road and run-over a coupla times too! I was like a pawn in their conniving chess game. I was going back 'a la naturale' Brown for sure! It was now so evident, why the many stares, as we were 'cordially seen together'…..in the minds of others we were a threesome alright….an intimate liaison of the unnatural kind!!!!!

I was grateful, particularly to my new Bestest Friends Ever, or so they thought!!! As I munched on the leftover, delicious, Lake food I felt an overwhelming sense of relief. We would have to see what morning would bring!

TIP: Don't you ever trust your Bestest Friends Ever….they'll turn out to be your Worstest Enemy
     FOREVER!!!!!
     Another little secret God wants you to know….Always trust your night cravin', or your
     intuitions…in one way or another, they'll do ya good every time!

RECIPES FOR:

Beguiling Peachy Sweet Tea   Out of the Ordinary Pound! Pound! Cake
Slitherin' Scoundrels String Potatoes/Cravin' for Fried Onion Rings
Hushpuppy Ho' Balls   Slippery Fish Fillets   What in Tarnation Turnip Greens
Deep Fried Dill Pickle Puss   Yummy Take to Church White Beans 'n Onions
Bestest Ever Fried Blonde Tomatoes

PW

LEFTOVERS

DEEP FRIED DILL PICKLE PUSS

Pat dry 2 16 oz jars dill pickle sandwich slices.....Beat 1 egg with 1 12 oz can beer   1 T baking powder   1 tsp salt
Add 1 ½ C all-purpose flour and blend 'til smooth
Pour canola oil about 2 inches deep in a fry skillet and heat on medium-high heat
Place the pickles in the batter, turning over and over to coat.....Fry the little dillies until golden ...Serve NOW!!

SLITHERIN' SCOUNDRELS STRING POTATOES

Peel 4 large sweet potatoes and cut them length-wise into long, skinny strips.....Deep-fry these GREAT FOR YA
sweeties then sprinkle with salt.....DIFFERENT AND DELICIOUS!!!

HUSHPUPPY HO' BALLS

Combine the following: 2 ¼ C self-risin white cornmeal   ½ chopped medium onion   ¼ tsp red pepper/black pepper
1 tsp salt   Stir in: 1 C buttermilk   2 lg eggs and let sit a few minutes
Drop these lil Ho balls by tablespoon into hot oil until golden brown and just watch em disappear, JUST LIKE BOB!

BESTEST EVER FRIED BLONDE TOMATOES

Cut 3 large green or yellow tomatoes into ¼ inch rounds....Drench them into the following mixture: 2 C self-risin flour
1 T garlic salt   2 T cajun seasoning
Fry in a skillet of hot canola oil for about 2 minutes each side...Drain and EAT THESE LITTLE DELIGHTS!

YUMMY TAKE TO CHURCH WHITE BEANS 'N ONIONS

Lightly saute ½ C chopped white onion until it turns a little brown....dump 1 lg can of Great Northern beans, half-drained,
on top the onions.....sprinkle with 1 tsp garlic pepper.....simmer about 15 minutes. Serve with some fresh chopped onion.

PW

WHAT IN TARNATION TURNIP GREENS

Wash 2 lb fresh turnip greens.....place them in a Dutch oven with:

8 slices bacon   3 peeled turnips   1 tsp sugar   ¼ tsp salt

Bring to a boil...reduce heat...simmer 20 minutes...stir then cook another 20 to 30 minutes...SOUTHERN TO THE CORE!

SLIPPERY FISH FILLETS

Place 6 6 oz catfish fillets in a shallow pan...cover with milk and chill 1 hour. Meantime combine: 2 C cornmeal

1 T seasoned salt   2 tsp pepper   ½ tsp onion powder   ½ tsp garlic powder   1 tsp salt

Take the fillets from the milk and dredge them in the cornmeal mixture.....Fry in deep canola oil about 4 minutes each side or until golden.....Drain and EAT 'EM HOT...OUT OF SIGHT!

CRAVIN' FOR FRIED ONION RINGS

Cut 3 large white onions in thick slices.....separate the rings.....soak them in: ½ C buttermilk   ½ C milk

Dredge em in 1 C flour.....redip into milk mixture then back into the flour.....Deep fry in canola oil.

OUT OF THE ORDINARY POUND! POUND! CAKE

Beat 1 lb butter and 3 C sugar until light and fluffy.....continue to beat in 6 large eggs and 2 tsp vanilla

Gradually blend in 4 C all-purpose flour and 1/3 C milk.....pour into a well greased Bundt pan.....

Bake at 325° for about 1 ½ hours.....when hot from the oven pour 1 C microwaved prepared Caramel icing all over.

NOBODY CAN RESIST THIS!!!

BEGUILING PEACHY SWEET TEA

Mix up 1 gallon store bought, good Peach Tea mix.....add 1 can citrus peach soda and 1 bottle peach nectar.....

Serve over lots of crushed ice with a fresh peach slice, a strawberry and a straw.....COOL!   COOL!   COOL!

PW

MAKE-A-MENDS BREAKFAST

Bob, the Dancing Fool, as he so admiringly called himself, almost became my new pet Fish....you know the one you bring home and it mysteriously dies the next day!!!! Sound crazy??? It is and ALWAYS was!!!!!

Before having little tadpoles, Bob and I would go dancing many a Saturday night. The auditorium would feature Greats like Ike and Tina Turner, Little Richard, Bo Diddly...and I mean in the Real! It was the 60's and you could catch their Fantastic Sounds as they traveled around the country, always getting booked to Boogie Down in Memphis, TN, the Home of the Blues.

Wherever we went, BoogieBob thought he was the best dancer in the room! WRONG! But, hey, I just let him think whatever...it usually saved a lot of wear 'n tear on my mind and body. This Saturday night, TwinkleToes Bob danced with every female and some males in the room, leaving them wondering what had just happened to 'em!!! The one dance I thankfully got with Bob, he kicked me in the head with his large, white, boat-of-an-Oxford, as he tried another new and unsuccessful dance step. I hit the floor and TippyToes just kept on movin', not even looking back.

Embarrassed and dizzy, I coaxed Bob from the dance with an ice-cold Beer I was using as an icepack. As I wearily drove us home, Bob sang every song he had heard which was a 'worst thing' than his dancing!!! We unlocked the door to home and Bob danced and sang his way in. Upon entering, FadingBob announced he wanted to soak his talented and aching body in a tub of steamy hot water. All I wanted to do was take two aspirin and lay the big knot coming up on my head, down on a soft pillow. My head was killin' me!!! Blurringly I heard BobbleBoy say, "Don't forget to get me outta here." I vaguely remember mumbling something like yea, sure, OK!

Low and behold, I DID FORGET!!! Later, MUCH later, like morning later, I patted the other side of the bed and there was NO BOB! I sat straight up on the kingsize square, saw sunlight, and heard the tweet tweet, of birds. Oh My GOSH!!! I had helped my husband drown himself!!! Not too shameful, I was thinking that wasn't a totally bad idea...self defense, battered wife, mentally-tortured spouse. Maybe I could plead the Left Alone Too Much Syndrome. The fact was, I had just been tired, sleepy, and had a whopping big knot on my noggin, a bump put there by You-Just-Had-To-Soak-In-A-Hot-Tub BOB!!!!

I snuck my way to the bathroom to find the old, Shriveled-Up Coot still sittin in the now, icy cold water, snoring through blue lips...arms crossed, and stuck under his armpits. I softly called his name cause I knew All Hell was about to break loose! He opened one eye, felt the coldness of the water, and jumped out screaming! Immediately, I saw he was still alive and well??? That same old shriveled thing was still peeking out like an undernourished raisin...Bob was definitely OK!

When The Man realized how long he had been soaking and what could have happened, he was FURIOUS WITH ME! I just crept to the kitchen smiling in my thoughts and fixed a fantastic breakfast fit for a King....a Dance King, a King of the Hot Tub.....the Artic Prune King??? Whatever King he thought himself to be that day I knew the night was still spinning in his head. Every once in a while I could see him shudder, maybe from thoughts of what could have been, or maybe he was still just Damn Cold!!! Yeah Baby!

TIP: Never dance with an embarrassing husband particularly if he wears size 12 shoes.
      If THEY insist on soakin', wait 5 minutes, pull the plug, cause they aren't gonna know anyway!!! OUT OF IT!!!

RECIPES FOR;

Icy Purple Blush   Dance King Coffee   Hot Tub Chocolate

Eggs Benedict with Dancindaise Sauce   BoogieBobs Garlic Cheese Grits   Prunes Soakin in Warm Sweet Milk

Fit-For-A-King Raisin Walnut Muffins with Blueberry Cream Cheese

PW

MAKE-A-MENDS BREAKFAST

ICY PURPLE BLUSH
In a blender mix: 1 lg frozen grape juice   1 small frozen orange juice   1 small frozen pineapple juice
1 handful frozen blueberries/raspberry mix   crushed ice
Pour in a pitcher with 1 very cold citrus soda.   EXCELLENT FOR SETTLIN' BOB'S SICK STOMACH.

HOT TUB CHOCOLATE
Just mix ya up a store-bought great hot chocolate drink....throw in some tiny marshmallows....dobble with whipped cream.
THAT'LL WAKE THE OLD BOY UP!

EGGS BENEDICT WITH DANCINDAISE SAUCE
Toast your favorite English muffin and butter lightly.....saute a slice of Canadian bacon then place on muffin.....top that
with a very thin slice of tomato.
Meantime you have boiled an egg and you've cut it into 3 neat slices.....place the 3 on top the tomato and smother with
THE sauce. Sauce recipe: beat 3 egg yolks until sticky   add 1 T lemon juice   1 T lime juice   pinch of salt and
beat for 1 ½ minutes   cook in a double boiler for 1 to 2 minutes until light and creamy
Beat in 1 T cold butter and pepper to taste. Pour over the piled-up muffin. LUSCIOUS!
THIS WILL GET A BOB TO DO ANYTHING!!!

BOOGIEBOB'S GARLIC CHEESE GRITS
Cook 1 C quick-cookin' grits as directed......add 1 Roll of garlic cheese and 1 stick butter   Combine 2 beaten eggs
with ¾ C milk   Pour the garlic mixture in a buttered baking dish then top with
Egg/milk mixture   Bake at 350°, uncovered for about 1 hour.
SOUTHERN! AND GRITS WILL GO WITH ANYTHING...ANYTIME!!!

PW

PRUNES SOAKIN' IN WARM SWEET MILK

Just soak ya about as many of these little wrinkles as you can eat in one breakfast.....ploop them in a
pretty lil bowl and pour about ¾ C microwaved milk over 'em.....let them swim abit. SO SWEET AND GOOD FOR YA!
NOTHING BETTER TO GET BOB BACK INTO DANCIN' SHAPE...HELL BE RUNNIN ALL MORNING!!!

FIT-FOR-A-KING RAISIN WALNUT MUFFINS

Beat all the following together for a Fantastic muffin that MIGHT BE TOO MOIST AND WHOLESOME FOR
AN OLD BOB!!!

½ C softened butter   1 C granulated sugar   2 lg eggs   1 lg banana   1 C chopped apples
2 C Whole Wheat flour   ¼ C Flax flour   1 tsp salt   1 tsp baking powder   1 tsp baking soda
1 ¼ C Buttermilk   ½ C chopped walnuts   ½ C raisins   2 tsp Vanilla

Spoon the batter into a heavily oiled 12 tin muffin pan   Bake at 375° for about 20 minutes
Serve warm with a prepared Blueberry or to-your-likin' Cream Cheese.   DREAMY GOOD!

PW

MAN'S USE-TO-BE BEST FRIEND

Brazen Bob had been such an Infidel lately that even our Border Collie, Rosey wasn't sure who he was! The kids just passed him off as somebody wanderin' through that they spoke to…..could have been the plumber!!! I never knew where the Wandering Bonehead gathered with his motley crew, I only heard he could be at This Place or That Place. What a comforting thought for a mother of two young children and a Border Collie.

I guess This Place or That Place didn't strike his fancy this particular night. Or maybe one of Bob's partners-in-crime couldn't get out of the house for the usual Rumps and Bumps, because HERE HE CAME….. home on a Friday night! With Blood-shot eyes and a Raggedy-Ass-Look, Bob headed toward our bedroom without so much as a grunt. Rosey recognized the scent and couldn't contain herself. She jumped all over him and licked his prickly stubble…ye gads…and acted as if she hadn't seen him in weeks. This was almost for real!

The two kinsmen trotted off to the bedroom….together. By this time in the relationship only a fellow dog would do the honors. I beg your pardon, this is not intended to disgrace the Real Canine families of the Earth. Bless their hearts, they are expected to act like despicable beasts, doggone it!!! As HereBob was about to close the two of them in the room I coldly informed him of the dinner he had missed yet again! The door slammed without a pant. From my new bedroom I could only imagine the scene…. nose to canine nose and snoring to unconsciously outdo each other. Poor Rosey! She was stuck for the night and loving it!! True dogs are so faithful…..no matter what!

Saturday morning came bright and early as usual but the sounds of the AM were by no means customary! I could hear the running of water both inside and outside the house, Rosey excitedly whelping, and Barking Bob howling orders to bet none! This I had to see!!! The washing machine was doing its thing on a load of sheets and poor old Rosie was in her bathing tin, covered with lather and bubbles. "WHAT'S THIS," I shouted in bewilderment! Bob exhaustedly said, "I noticed Rosey had fleas all over her." "You're crazy…. I just had Her bathed and groomed at the Vets yesterday," I disgustedly replied.

I searched high and low for the 'Flea' soap and finally found it hidden among the dirty towels. After examining the label, I gasped in disbelief!!! The doggone Beastie Bob had given his own dog the CRABS!!!! He had just disappointed and disgraced the only friend he had left in the house!

TIP: Keep your Pets away from unsightly characters! When the Bob-of-the-House continuously goes This Place and That Place, always without you.....it is time for you to go to the New Somewhere Else Place without him!

PW

RECIPES FOR:

Beastie Bobs

Rumps 'n Bumps Southern Crab Soup   Crusty Friendship Rolls

Rosemary Grilled Pork Chops   Stuffed Squash-the-Crabbies

This or That Places Lemony Cheesecake Pie

MAN'S USE-TO-BE BEST FRIEND

RUMPS 'N BUMPS SOUTHERN CRAB SOUP
Boil together ALL the following: 1 can Cheddar cheese soup   1 can cream of celery soup   3 C milk
   1 C half 'n half   ½ C butter   2 chopped hard-boiled eggs   ½ tsp Worcestershire   ½ tsp garlic salt
   ½ tsp pepper   1 ½ C crab meat   ½ C dry sherry   Cook on LOW for 30 minutes and serve....YUM!

CRUSTY FRIENDSHIP ROLLS
SIMPLE! Purchase a bag of small sour dough breads.....split them down the middle and fill with garlic butter
Heat until crusty for the best taste...Dip it in the soup!

ROSEMARY GRILLED PORK CHOPS
Purchase those thick large pork chops.....cut little slivers into the meat and insert small fresh garlic pieces.....
Crush 1 T fresh rosemary and combine with 1 tsp seasoned salt/pepper.....place the chops in 1 C white and
½ C canola oil.....sprinkle with the rosemary mixture and simmer until cooked...about 45 minutes...watch the liquids
and baste often...but not to throw off the rosemary.....that's what gives it the GREAT TASTE!!!

STUFFED SQUASH-THE-CRABBIES
Combine ALL the following then plop into a greased baking dish to bake at 400° for 30 minutes:
4 C uncooked, sliced, unpeeled zucchini   ½ C canola oil   1 ½ C shredded sharp cheese   1 ½ C powdered biscuit mix
     1 10 oz can crabmeat   3 eggs   1 C Chopped onion   1 tsp oregano   1 tsp salt/pepper
                    SO CRABBY DELICIOUS!

PW

THIS OR THAT PLACE'S LEMONY CHEESECAKE PIE
Bake 2 prepared piecrusts at 400° for 5 minutes...poke a few holes around the crusts before bakin'.....
Beat together 2 8 oz cream cheese, 1 egg, ½ C sugar.....Spread in bottom of pie crusts.....Prepare 1 box lemon chess
pie filling according to direction and pour over 1st layer.....Bake at 350 for about 30 minutes.....pile with whipped cream.

THE MOTHERLOAD

Travelin' Bob was just arriving home from yet another lengthy business trip. "You'd think people could find an attorney in their own town," Marcie naively thought! Being such a trustin' soul, Marcie had a hard time catching on to Bobby's dubious shenanigans! But, she was finally 'getting the drift'. After each of his journeys, she found 'extras items' in Bob's suitcase and she was even beginning to think three and four day trips, three or four times a month a bit too excessive!

Well, after depositing his bags by the front door, BlusteringBob ran upstairs to change into his golf clothes for his usual tee time. As he sprang for the door, Bob hurriedly asked, "What's for dinner? Whatever it is let's have some of the GOOD WINE," rubbing his chubby hands together and licking his 'can-ya-guess-where-I've-been' lips. He turned his useless back and slammed the door. Marci begrudgingly started totin' the bags upstairs, thinking she should leave 'em for him to clear.....but of course they might sit there for a week and instinct was telling this Blondie to SEIZE and SEARCH!

WOW, and double WOW, the MOTHERLOAD materialized before her startled eyes.....BIGGER THAN LIFE.....different erotic condoms, worn silky, sexy panties, contraptions of all sorts, and PICTURES, lewd, vulgar photos of TigerBob and his Pussycat in various disgusting positions. The Feline Seducer had probably stashed these incriminating props just as Tiger had closed his Toy Bag. Wifey Poo would surely find them as she, like only a good wife would do, helped her busy husband unpack! As she picked up his suit jacket to throw it across the room, Marci felt a heaviness, not only in her heart, but in the pocket. There they were, stamped roundtrip tickets to Miami Beach, FL. WELL, WELL, WELL!!! Either Bob was as Dumb-as-a-Post or he was in on the stashing!!!

Livid and revengeful, Marci came up with a sinister plan. She filled a pan with hot, sudsy detergent and stormed with it to the basement. A dark cool portion was designated as, BOB'S WINERY. "Yes, my Sexy husband, we will have some of the GOOD, expensive wine for dinner," Marcie devilishly laughed! A vast and expensive collection lay before her just waiting to be turned again or opened and lavishly consumed, just like the bodies in the photos! The MOST expensive and hard to find bottles, that had made their way from regions all over the world, now found their way to Marcie's lowly soap pan.

Soon, each astute, carefully designed Label was floating like the Titanic! Marci carefully took each bottle, wiped it clean and opened every last SNOB-of-a-bottle to reveal the lavish and rich nose! To Marci, these strong garnet-like liquids had musty bouquets of smelly, dirty socks and the taste of 'em too! Yuk!

She gathered her soon-to-be-ruined loot to the upstairs kitchen table and posed each of the fifty bottles around the Kitty and Tiger poses. Red eyes gleaming, Marci then placed the raw food that would have become a scrumptious dinner, around the revolting stash. MY, MY, the array looked just like a Food/Wine section of that Hot, Sexy, Porn Magazine!!

So proud of her artistic spread and her new-found awareness, Marci packed her bags and air-kissed her interesting display good-bye. This Blondie was hoppin' the last one-way flight to New Orleans.....First Class!

TIP: Always go through your so-called partner's luggage...ALWAYS...don't wait for intuition to kick you in the booty!
       Every time you're smellin' and sippin' those 'dirty sock' wines, give a little cheer to all the Marcis of the world!!!!!

RECIPES FOR:

Shenanigan My Ass Again Mango Bongos
(for the flight)
A RED AND WHITE WINE LIST IS PROVIDED   PW

OH BABY!

I was lying in the Hospital bed after having delivered a ten-pound Bundle of Joy less than twenty-four hours earlier. I groggily looked up to the Television when, low and behold, I see my Prince Charming strollin' across the screen!!! "What...What is This," I asked of my hurting self? GoofyGolfin Bob had hightailed it to the ProAm Golf Tournament at the Country Club!

I couldn't believe my eyes, and I absolutely couldn't believe DaddyO was stuffin' his mouth with a huge Burger and guzzling a frothy Beer. If that wasn't enough to handle, he also had his hairy arm around a Hot Patootie that was dressed in a way-too- small halter top and cheek-showin' short shorts!!! Dang It, the camera moved to scan the crowd and I lost sight of the ditsy duo just as LoverBoy started nibbling Shorties ear!!!

You would have thought the no-good, low-down, fast talkin', cheatin' JackASS hadn't eaten in days. Of course, he probably hadn't. I WAS IN THE HOSPITAL HAVIN' HIS BABY!!!

TIP: Some Bob's are not worth 'Tits on a Boar Hog!'

RECIPES FOR:

    Double Whammy on Rye   Nerd Nacho Grande   Dork Burgers
      MeatHead Meatball Subs   Hide-the-Winnie Hotdogs

LC

OH BABY!   LC

DOUBLE WHAMMY ON RYE

Rye cocktail bread slices   hot pepper sauce   bulk pork sausage   American cheese. Fry sausage and drain grease. Add American cheese. Add hot pepper sauce to taste.   Spread on bread slices. Broil until bubbly. This little number could turn your CHEEKS red if you over do the HOT STUFF !

NERD NACHO GRANDE

1 large bag...nacho chips   1 lb. hamburger meat   1 can refried beans   1 finely chopped onion   1 pack taco sauce mix   1 C shredded cheddar cheese   1 small head shredded lettuce   1 diced tomato   ½ C diced hot peppers   ½ C diced black olives.. Brown   hamburger....onion ......drain... add taco sauce mix. Spread chips on   baking pan...layer refried beans...hamburger...cheese. Bake till cheese melts. Garnish... lettuce, tomato, hot peppers; black olives.   NIBBLE to your hearts content, it may be awhile till this HOT PATOOTIE comes around again !

DORK BURGERS

1 ½ lbs ground beef   1 medium onion, finely chopped   1 C dry bread crumbs   1/3 C grated Parmesan cheese   2/3 C pine nuts   ¼ C chopped fresh parsley   2 eggs   1 ½ t salt   1 t pepper. Combine all ingredients; blend well. Shape into 6 thick patties. Grill patties on covered grill, 5 minutes each side or until done. STUDMUFFIN STUFFIN BURGER !

MEATHEAD MEATBALL SUBS

1 (1 ¼ lb) package fresh ground turkey   ¼ C plain yogurt   ½ C chopped green onions   1/3 C finely crumbed toast 1 large tomato, peeled, seeded and chopped   2 T grated Parmesan cheese   ¼ t garlic salt   1 t butter   1 clove garlic, finely chopped   ¼ t vegetable seasoning   8 C chopped fresh spinach. Mix turkey, yogurt, green onion, toast crumbs, tomato, Parmesan cheese and garlic salt. Shape into 1 ½ inch balls. Place in shallow baking pan. Bake 20 minutes at 350 ° or until turkey is no longer pink. Heat butter in saucepan. Add garlic clove and vegetable seasoning. Stir in spinach; cook until limp. Place meatballs and spinach on large serving platter, pour excess juice from meatballs over top. Serve with crusty sub buns. BOB'S BUNS WERE ALWAYS SUB !

HIDE-THE-WINNIE HOTDOGS

8 frankfurters   1 C bread crumbs   1 T minced onion   1 t melted butter   ¼ t salt   pepper   8 slices bacon. Split frankfurters partly lengthwise. Combine bread crumbs, onions, butter, salt and pepper. Add boiling water to moisten. Fill mixture in opening of frankfurter. Wrap bacon around each frankfurter and broil until bacon is crisp. LITTLE WINKIE BOB LOVED WINNIES !

PARADISE LOST

The Gulf Coast in Summertime was a delightful place for a Vacation. Its warm, crystal-clear, Emerald waters, soft ocean breeze, powdery sugar, white sand, and beautiful Sunsets make you think you're in Heaven…..unless of course, you are with Bob! He would always make it like your Worst Nightmare in living color!!!

All day he would sit on the beach, under his Big ol' Umbrella, sippin his Coolers, NOT missin' a single solitary Fanny, that was barely draped in itty, bitty Thongs! Sex Kittens were all over the Beach, floutin' their seemingly available, bodacious 'tatas' in a rainbow of gorgeous colors……gaudy vermilion, hot pinks and reds, flashy yellows and greens, sky blues, and of course, the infamous midnight black!!! ALL, to torture the mother of three, with her less than perky boobs and not-so-flat tummy! Yeks…..WHY the Beach??? BobbyBoobs was in Seventh Heaven!!!

Something was always UP with Bob and this time was no different. I knew it was comin' when the DoNothin' Ever offered to get the towels from the Laundry dryer. IT took him an hour to get back to the Condo and the Laundry was right below! He was sweatin' bullets, breathin' like a freight train, and his swimming trunks were on BACKWARDS! Something had been UP all right!!!

I just looked at him, shook off the sand, and went about preparing a scrumptious, fresh Seafood Feast of lump crab, and grilled Red Snapper. You know, MachoMan Bob always loved a good Snapper!

TIP: Rent a vacation Condo that has its own Washer and Dryer.

RECIPES FOR:

Rainbow Mango Margaritas	Strawberry Afternoon Delight	French Peach Fizz
Grilled Red Snapper	West Indies Crab Salad	Sleazy Cheesy Zucchini Sneaky Pete Cornbread

PARADISE LOST

RAINBOW MANGO MARGARITAS
See LIBATION RECIPES at the end of the book

STRAWBERRY AFTERNOON DELIGHT

8 large strawberries with leaves   1 (6-oz) package semisweet chocolate chips, melted $\frac{1}{2}$ C chilled whipping cram 1 T cherry brandy. Dip strawberries $\frac{3}{4}$ of the way in chocolate; place on waxed paper, refrigerate 30 minutes. Beat together cream and brandy. Divided cream mix.... 4 dishes, top each with 2 chocolate-dipped strawberries. EAT THEM ALL YOUR-SELF !

FRENCH PEACH FIZZ
See LIBATION RECIPES at the end of the book

GRILLED RED SNAPPER

$\frac{1}{2}$ C butter melted $\frac{1}{4}$ C lemon juice   2 C bread crumbs   1 T chopped parsley $\frac{1}{2}$ t paprika   1 lb fresh red snapper. Combine butter and lemon juice. Combine bread crumbs, parsley and $\frac{1}{4}$ C of lemon mixture. Add paprika to remaining lemon mixture. Dip fish into paprika mixture. Grill under broiler until fish flakes with fork. Top with bread crumb mixture. Return to broiler and heat through until warm. There are bigger fish to fry, some you could put a saddle on and ride 'em. FISHY BOBBER CAN HOOK SOME BIG ONES !

WEST INDIES CRAB SALAD

1 lb. of lump crabmeat, picked of all loose shell $\frac{1}{2}$ C light vegetable oil $\frac{1}{2}$ C red wine vinegar $\frac{1}{2}$ C iced water (drain ice from water so that you have $\frac{1}{2}$ C of actual water)   dash of salt   heavy dash of black pepper   dash of artificial sweetener   1 large red onion...chopped medium fine. In the bottom of a covered dish with a tight lid...add $\frac{1}{2}$ chopped onion, 1 lb. crabmeat; other $\frac{1}{2}$ chopped onion. Add in this order...oil, vinegar, water. Sprinkle salt, pepper; sweetener. Chill 24 hours... stir before serving. Serve with cracked pepper crackers. Double dog dare you not to love this crabby delicious salad !

SLEAZY CHEESY ZUCCHINI

1/3 C cornflake crumbs   2 T grated Parmesan cheese   ½ t seasoned salt   garlic powder   4 small unpeeled zucchini, cut in 3 ½-in strips   ¼ C melted butter. Combine cornflake crumbs, cheese and seasonings. Dip zucchini strips in butter then coat with crumb mixture. Bake 10 minutes at 375 ° or until crisp. A tough act to follow !

SNEAKY PETE CORNBREAD

1 (1 lb) can cream-style corn   ¾ C milk   1/3 C butter   1 C cornmeal   2 eggs, slightly beaten   ½ t baking soda   1 t baking powder   1 (4-oz) can green chilies   1 ½ C shredded cheddar cheese. Mix all ingredients together. Pour into greased 9-inch square pan. Bake 45 minutes at 400 ° until golden brown. Serve piping hot. SNEAKY BOB, SNEAKY JOHN, SNEAKY JAKE, SNEAKY SNAKE IN THE GRASS.......

LC

PREACHER MAN

Good, faithful Preacher Bob had it made; a beautiful family, a wealthy church right in the middle of ski country, a million dollar house on the side of a snow covered mountain, and a cute little sweetie to boot! Plus, the kids were away at college, and both extended families lived back East. Could life get any better???

Jeannie, Bob's devoted wife, often took trips back home and to visit the children at school. These frequent trips added to Bible Bob's good life. While she was gone and no family to be accountable to, Bob and his weekly Bible Study Co-leader, Sue MacIvy, GOT IT ON!!! The getting got good in the Ski Resorts, on the biking trails, and in the Church Van with the mountains bikes. Their lustful liaisons even transpired in the minister's OWN SANCTUARY, probably in the baptismal!! But, this Holier-than-Thou, ceremonial immersion was of the Hellfire, Damnation kind! THE UTTER SHAME OF IT!!! If that wasn't enough slap in the face to the Moralizer's calling, the worst sacrilege of all was the carnal acts committed in the Preacher Man's OWN BED, in his OWN HOUSE, on his OWN 600 count white cotton sheets!!! And such licentiousness right in front of the kid's old dog, Maggie!!!

Well, Elmer Bob and his poisonous companion, SueMac, thought their indiscretions were unique little secrets, although the congregation had been suspecting this infidelity for sometime. But not one Snow Bunny was willing to 'cast the first stone'! So, this unprecedented love affair grew as Jeannie's Frequent Flyer Miles increased.

But, as we know, even the tingling itch of poison Ivy comes to an end at some point. Little did the two Illicit Irritants know, the Good Wife had caught wind of the 'wild tails' and had begun putting two and two together. Was this why the crowds grew for the Bible Studies…the glow of infidelity was creating charisma??? Or is this why Missionary Bob was so very agreeable about her frequent trips??? Or was this why new sheets were always on their bed when she arrived home???

Well now, Doubting Jeannie decided to make the trip of her lifetime!!! Preacher took her to the airport as usual, lovingly gave his wife a hug, and left before the plane boarded. "I just have to prepare for tomorrow nights Bible Study," he seriously said. Jeannie was counting on this. She never boarded that plane bound for the East. When she waited enough time for Preacher Man to have left the area, she rented a car and stayed out of sight for the rest of the day. She was betting SueMac and BibleBob were doin' their preparing for that mini sermon on the Israelites leaving Egypt, at the parsonage.

She parked below their house so the car lights wouldn't shine on the new snow, as if they would be looking anyway! Once Jeannie saw the only lights shining upstairs, she crept through the garage entrance and quietly greeted Maggie. They tiptoed to the living room hideaway where both creatures were forced to listen to the 'parting of the Red Sea' taking place in her own bedroom in her own bed!!! Grossed out and humiliated, Jeannie knew the battle would reach a climax soon, so she and Maggie sat in wait, and waited, and waited. Sure enough, VICTORY could be heard! Just as she anticipated, hunger and thirst always abide after a great battle. Here the lovers came to the kitchen. Jeannie was ready!

Naked as jaybirds, the two victors emerged from the 'study area,' bouncing and cheering triumphantly. But, their victory quickly turned to defeat! Sitting at the dining table was the Betrayed, the Enemy, but TRUE CONQUERORS, the wife and faithful old dog, Maggie! Jeannie slyly asked, "Would anyone like drinks and a snack???"

Needless to say, there were no more Bible Studies, at least not led by Preacher Man and the Creeping Vine. And, the next trip back East was permanent for Jeannie and her true, devoted companion, Maggie.

TIPS: Attach a tiny video camera to your dogs collar next time you're goin' out-of-town.
       Always keep a great pair of trackin' boots in the trunk of your car...you may need them sooner than you think!

PW

PUSHY POOL PARTY

Summertime and the livin' was easy, for some folks anyway.....and then there was Bob, who could mess-up a One Car Funeral! When he occasionally showed up at Home, he'd be ready to Preach a Sermon and make Big Productions out of NOTHING! Jack, Ginger, Crystal, and Yours Truly were lambasted everyday for not having 'All Our Ducks In A Row'.....I hate ducks to this very day!!! BobADoodleDo thought of himself as God's Gift to Humanity.....the kids and I secretly called him GodsZilla!

One lovely, Southern Summer night, I exhaustedly came Home from work, all dressed in my attractive frilly frock and cute little sling pumps. GodsZilla was comfortably lounging in the backyard by the Pool. I surely must have said SOMETHIN' wrong, because one minute I was, with clinched jaws, smiling pleasantly and sashaying across the Patio, but in a flash, I was gasping for breath and screamin' for HELP!!! The Jerk had downed a few-too-many and went totally ballistic, tossing me into the deep-end of the Pool like a sack of potatoes!

Devilish Bonehead Bob was laughing like a JackASS while I was trying to keep from drowning! Thank Goodness I had put a Corned Beef in the Crock-pot that morning or our dinner would have been a disaster!!!

TIP: Do your kids a favor.....DO NOT stay married for their sake.....you could destroy their feelings for Feathered Fowl
       of ALL SPECIES. Always keep a life-preserver handy.....with or without a Pool.

RECIPES FOR:

Crackpot Crock-pot Corned Beef   Bonehead Bean Salad
Crazy Carrots with New Potatoes
Salted Nut-Head Cake   Spiced-Up Tea

LC

PUSHY POOL PARTY   LC

CRACKPOT CROCK-POT CORN BEEF

2 lbs corned beef brisket   1 small onion, quartered   1 clove garlic, crushed   1 small head cabbage, cut into 6 wedges. Place corned beef in crock pot, cover with water. Add onion and garlic. Heat to boiling; reduce heat. Simmer until beef is tender, about 2 hours. Remove beef to warm platter. Skim fat from broth. Add cabbage; heat to boiling. Reduce heat and simmer 15 minutes. Will warm you up after a few laps in the pool !

BONEHEAD BEAN SALAD

1 (16-oz) can kidney beans   1 (16-oz) can pinto beans   1 (16-oz) can garbanzo beans   1 (16-oz) can unsalted whole-kernel corn $\frac{1}{2}$ C green onions, chopped $\frac{1}{4}$ C chopped parsley   1 C sliced celery. Drain and rinse beans and corn. Combine all ingredients. Add dressing and mix well. Chill overnight.   For dressing, mix together: 4 T olive oil   2 cloves garlic, minced 1 t oregano leaves $\frac{1}{2}$ t cumin and curry mixture $\frac{1}{2}$ t pepper $\frac{3}{4}$ C vinegar $\frac{1}{2}$ t sugar. Mix ingredient together.... Pour over the vegetables. Chill over night. Go jump in the lake has taken on a whole new meaning, you know what I mean ?

CRAZY CARROTS WITH NEW POTATOES

6 long carrots chunky cut   12 new potatoes   salt to taste   pepper to taste $1\frac{1}{2}$ C shredded cheddar cheese   1 C bacon bits   3 T chopped pimiento $\frac{1}{2}$ C melted butter. Boil carrots and potatoes until tender. Slice potatoes in half. Spray baking dish with butter flavored non-stick spray...arrange potatoes and carrots in checker-board design. Salt... pepper slightly....top with pimiento, bacon bits, shredded cheese. Drizzle with melted butter. Bake in 350° oven 5 minutes   till cheese   melts. Easy as falling off a log !

SALTED NUT-HEAD CAKE

$1\frac{3}{4}$ C cake flour   1 t soda $\frac{1}{2}$ t salt   1 C sugar $\frac{1}{2}$ C buttery shortening   2 eggs   1 C buttermilk   1 jar drained maraschino cherries $1\frac{1}{2}$ C crushed salted nuts. Cream shortening...add sugar...beaten eggs. Sift flour... soda...salt. Slowly, add flour mixture to sugar shortening mixture, stirring in buttermilk. Add 1 C nuts, stir gently. Bake in 325° oven ... 45 minutes... bake ... greased   9 inch round   pan. Top with white icing.... $\frac{1}{2}$ C   salted nuts...maraschino cherries. A   NUT-CRUNCHING   END   TO   A   SWIMMINGLY   EVENTFUL EVENING !

SPICED-UP TEA

Prepare lemon flavored tea mix according to package directions...add cranberry juice cocktail...lemon slice... dash of cinnamon. Serve over crushed ice.

RIPPIN' BRITCHES

Sleep was so sweet until a heavy flop onto the bed startled me back to reality. Long ago I learned, like Pavlovs dog, to assume nothing, say nothing, just do what you know. So without investigation, and to the tune of Bob's moans and groans, I went back to my dreams.

When the light of day crept into my eyes, I hit the floor, stumbling over a heap of Late Night Bob's clothing. As usual, I gathered the bundle, dumped them into the basket, but not without examination. Must have been SOME activity last night, I thought! Body Odor Bob's shirt was smellier than usual, prickled with tiny red dots, and as wet as a training athlete. That in itself let me know there was a snake in the woodpile! Bob's new suit pants had a huge gaping rip that was decorated with what looked like blood! YEK! What had this JackAss been up to???

"Robert...Bob...oh, Bobby Boy," I called, but there was no answer. He had already left??? Well, I had no time to ponder this present shenanigan, I needed to get goin to decorate the room for our Garden Club Luncheon. When I entered the Club, gossip was rippin around the room as damaging as the rip in Broken Bob's pants! "Lawdy mercy ladies, let me in on this, I need a good diversion," I shouted over the crowd!

Seems there was quite a raucous in Cindilou's neighborhood last night. Some Loverboy jumped fences for a late night rendezvous in his lover's backyard. Just as the hot summer night got a lot steamier, and things were movin' right along on a flimsy lawn chair, the unexpected husband pulled into the driveway. Sweaty bodies flew at the sound sending somebody's wife to the concrete and somebody's husband back over the fences, quicker than a jackrabbit! On his way over, the aging Casanova ripped a portion out of his pants and fell into the neighbors thick rose garden! Muffled human cries and yelps from nearby dogs could be heard clear across the yards. I guarantee you, these neighbors would keep this story alive for years!!!

I was hilariously aghast by this shamefully funny episode even though it was definitely beginning to hit TOO CLOSE TO HOME!!! I hated to miss the delicious Luncheon, but I excused myself...I had some decorating to do on my own! I hurried home knowing this was another 'tail' of Bob's indiscretion and I needed to let my amorous adventurer know I had become aware of his not-to-well-hidden secret! So...I decided to have a Pioneer Washday!!!

I took every suit from JackaBob's closet, and believe me, there were lots of 'um. I drew scalding hot water in the outside dog tub and scrubbed every last one of them with the harshest soap I could muster up! Then I took each lovely, DRY CLEAN ONLY, piece and very neatly threw them across the fence to Sun Dry!!! Oh, the sunshine made them all have pretty new colors, and the good ol hot water shrunk them down to the size fit for a little boy.....just like Cheatin Bob really was!

TIP: Always keep one of those soaps around that nobody uses anymore cause it eats off your skin. You never know when you might have to wash some JackAsses clothes!

RECIPES FOR:

Bloody JackaBobs

Casanova Salmon Croquettes   Scrubbed Lil' Potatoes Prickled with Parsley

Steamed Asparagus Foldovers   Sun Dried Tomato Salad

Pioneer Puddin' Tarts   Banana Split-Your-Pants Pie

PW

122

RIPPIN BRITCHES

CASANOVA SALMON CROQUETTES
Mix well together: 1 16 oz can Salmon   ½ C chopped onion   2/3 C dry bread crumbs
2 beaten eggs   1 tsp dillweed   ½ tsp dry mustard
Shape into patties and cook in 2 T Canola oil until brown on both sides...about 3 minutes

SCRUBBED LIL POTATOES PRICKLED WITH PARSLEY
Peel a band around the middle of 3 lb small new potatoes.....Boil about 20 minutes.....Drain
Meantime: melt 2 T butter   blend in 2 T flour   1 tsp minced garlic   1 tsp Cajun seasoning   1 C milk
1 C shredded American cheese   Mix well then.....Ploop in your lil potatoes and stir .
Sprinkle with ¼ C fresh chopped Parsley   GREAT SIDE DISH!

STEAMED ASPARAGUS FOLDOVERS
Take the sides off a loaf of White bread.....flatten the slices between wax paper.....generously butter and
Sprinkle with Parmesan cheese.....drain a large can of good Asparagus stems.....pat dry with paper towel.
Place a stem in the corner of each slice then roll up.....place seam down on a buttered cookie sheet and
Bake for 10 to 12 minutes at 400°.....from the oven, sprinkle with more Parmesan.
SO YUMMY AND MAKES BOB THINK HE'S SPECIAL!

SUN DRIED TOMATO SALAD
Use a bag of Spring mix lettuce.....wash and dry before placing in a salad bowl.....Using your kitchen sheers,
Snipe the sun-dried tomatoes into bite-sized pieces right onto the lettuce..... Add a handful of sun-dried raisins.....
A handful of chopped, salted pecans.....½ C chopped purple onion.....½ C mixed chopped yellow/red peppers.....
1 C garlic whole wheat croutons......½ C real bacon.....Mix together with a light prepared Caesar Salad dressin'
Sprinkle with a grated Romano cheese......   PW
THOSE LIL RAISINS AND TOMATOES FEEL JUST LIKE BOB'S CLOTHES.....OH, TOO BAD!

BANANA SPLIT-YOUR-PANTS PIE

Mix 2 C graham cracker crumbs with 1 melted stick of butter.....spread on the bottom of a 9 X 13 pan.

Combine: 3 C confectioners sugar   1 8 oz cream cheese   1 tsp vanilla   1 egg   Spread on crust.

Add a layer of sliced bananas over that layer and then 1 can drained crushed pineapple.....Top with a nondairy
whipped topping and sprinkle with ½ C chopped walnuts or pecans.....refrigerate at least 12 hours.

WAY TOO GOOD FOR BOB!

PIONEER PUDDIN TARTS

Add all the following together: 1 C sugar   2 eggs   1 stick butter   dash of salt

1 tsp vanilla   1 C oatmeal   1 C corn syrup

Blend well and pour into unbaked tart crusts or 1 unbaked pie crust.....Bake at 350° for 45 minutes if a pie
crust is used.....much less time for the tarts.....you'll know when the center is firm.

Dollop with Vanilla whipped toppin' or Vanilla Ice Cream

PW

124

SHAKE, RATTLE, AND RUN

Steamroller Bob would drag in after midnight, drunk as a Boiled Owl, and stumble though the kitchen, bouncing off the walls, and cussing a Blue Streak! Robert's colorful use of the English language could astound the most raucous, low-life JackASS this side of the River! In fact, he might have been a 'Closet Rapper' in disguise! Of course, according to Bob, he was selling Spirits to the local Night Spots and it was his job to SERVICE his accounts. I am quite sure he pecked around all night, Servicing 'STUFF'!

The bedrooms in our house were on the second floor and the kids had a habit of just droppin' their shoes at the bottom of the stairs. God help them if LateNight Stumblin' PeckerHead Bob spotted a flip-flop laying around! He would gleefully crawl and claw his way to the top, depositing foot-ware of every description in bed with his children. That, of course, would begin a chain reaction of whoopin' and hollerin' enough to wake the dead! Cruel DaddyBob was a throw-back to the Barbarian Age. One thing for sure, he did get the Show on the Road.....everyone would be cryin' and callin' for Mommy while their drunken, carousing father tried to 'pat my fanny'.....I would rather have JAWS as a bed partner!

Running like a chicken with it's head cut off, I would race from room to room consoling the children. Drunk-as-a-skunk, Bob would pass out cold while I fumed the rest of the night. A good lawyer could probably plead me Insane if I had gone on and shot him, but I couldn't take the chance!

Bright and early I dashed to the kitchen and started rattlin' those pots and pans...there was a whole lot of shakin' goin on! The oven door slammed loud enough to wake the dead or a snoring Bull Elephant. Headachin' Bob came runnin' down the stairs like a ravin' maniac in a Looney Bin, spoutin' orders with his usual Loudmouth Self! I calmly and deadly told him I was fixin' breakfast.....he raised his hand and gave me a sign that instantly let me know he wouldn't be eating with us. Oh Darn!

I really gotta learn to talk better with my fingers.....it takes a person with Super Intelligence to communicate so effectively without opening their mouth!

TIP; Persevere!   Learn sign language.

RECIPES FOR:

Belly-Up-To-The-Bar Puffy Pancakes

Swiss Kick Turkey Quiche   Ego Egg Bake   Beer Joint Muffins

LC

PW

SHAKE, RATTLE, AND RUN   LC

BELLY-UP-TO-THE-BAR PUFFY PANCAKES

2 eggs   4 large potatoes peeled and grated   1 t salt   1/8 t black pepper   1 T flour   2 T minced parsley   ¼ C minced green onions   butter   sour cream. Beat eggs until thick; combine with potatoes. Add salt and pepper, flour, parsley and onions. Drop by tablespoon into hot butter. Sauté till crisp around edges and brown on both sides. Drain on paper towels and serve very hot with sour cream. RAPPER RAMBO ROBERT BELLIED UP WITH THE BEST OF 'EM, AT ANY BAR HE COULD FIND!!

SWISS KICK TURKEY QUICHE

1 (9-inch) unbaked pie crust   1 C cut up turkey   1 C shredded Swiss cheese   ½ C sliced mushrooms   4 eggs   2 C half and half   ¾ t salt   ¼ t pepper. Sprinkle turkey, cheese and mushrooms in pie crust. Beat eggs slightly; beat in half-and-half, salt and pepper; pour into pie crust. Bake at 425 ° for 15 minutes. Reduce temperature to 300 ° and bake an additional 30 minutes. Let stand 10 minutes before cutting. INSANELY DEVINE KICK START FOR ANOTHER FLIP-FLOPPING DAY !

EGO EGG BAKE

1/3 C butter   ½ C flour   ½ t salt   dash white pepper   2 C milk   2 C grated American or Swiss cheese   6 eggs   6 slices hot toast. Melt butter in skillet; stir in four, salt and white pepper to make a smooth paste. Stir in milk, cooking over low heat until smooth and thick. Blend in 1 cup cheese, stirring until smooth. Pour cheese sauce into a greased casserole. Break eggs in sauce dish and slip into sauce at regular intervals. Sprinkle eggs with remaining cheese. Bake covered for 20 minutes at 325°, uncover and cook 5 minutes longer. Serve over hot toast. This dish will make you CRACK a smile.

BEER JOINT MUFFINS

3 C biscuit mix   3 T sugar   1 can beer. Mix ingredients; spoon into greased muffin tin. Bake 30 minutes at 400°. Buy a 6 pack, make muffins with one and drink the rest!

SUNDAY DINNER

Sundays should be relaxing, restful days that families spend together enjoying each other.....kinda like the old movies where the Mother always wore heels while dustin' the furniture, and the Dad had a smile on his face as he washed the car in his suit. In our house everyone would put on their Sunday-Go-To-Meetin' Clothes, joyfully pile into our big Sedan, and off to Church we would go to join the rest of the congregation in Song and Praise.....YEAH, RIGHT!!!

Righteous Robert would wake up like an angry Gorilla ready to snap someones head off....usually it was Jacks or mine! All the children were in tears when we piled in the car, and I had already told Bob where to stick it at least ten times! Fortunately, the kids would manage to pull it together by the time we reached the church parking lot and I had offered lots of silent prayers asking the Good Lord to help me through one more Sunday dinner without feedin' the man poison mushrooms!!!

Pious Bob, in his fancy pinstripe suit, would lead the way as we marched in like Happy wooden soldiers.....nobody knew we had already been to War!!! Everyone would nod and smile at the seemingly Happy Family as we would grit our teeth, nod, and grin like possums.

After Services the weary kindred would head home to Sunday dinner, the highlight of the day. I prepared the salad, sliced the roast, arranged the vegetables artfully on the platter, and baked the bread.....all the while cussing like the best Sailor, of course, under my breath. Jack and Ginger would set the table while JackASS changed into something more comfortable.....a Monkey Suit would have been my suggestion!

TIP: There is no such thing as a Free Lunch!

RECIPES FOR:

       PotShot Pot Roast   Make My Day Salad   Heavenly Bread   Hot Mama Pepper Jelly
          Rock 'Em, Sock 'Em Carrots, Potatoes and Mushrooms   Cocktail Cake

LC

SUNDAY DINNER   LC

POTSHOT POT ROAST

5 lbs chuck roast with bone   ½ t salt   ¼ t pepper   1 T beef base   1 C tomato juice   2 cloves minced garlic
1 large onion, chopped   3 stalks celery, chopped   water. Place roast in 2 ½-quart baking dish; sprinkle with salt, pepper and beef base. Add garlic, onion and celery. Pour tomato juice over top and add water to cover beef. Cover and bake at 350 ° for 3 hours. Use juice of beef to thicken for gravy. Yummy....even wooden soldiers like pot roast.

MAKE MY DAY SALAD

2 C (1/2 small head) shredded lettuce   2 C (1 bunch) torn spinach   1 C (1/2 head) ½-in slices cauliflower florets
1 C (1/2 medium) ½-in sliced unpeeled zucchini   1 C (2 small) chopped tomatoes   1 C (4 oz) strips sharp cheddar cheese   ½ C (1/2 small) red onion rings, separated. In large bowl, toss together all ingredients. Cover, chill 1 -2 hours. Serve with favorite dressing.

HEAVENLY BREAD

1 package active dry yeast   1 ¼ C warm water   2 T honey   2 T butter   1 t salt   3 C flour. Dissolve yeast in water; stir in honey. Add butter, salt and 2 C flour; mix well. Add remaining flour. Grease dough, cover and let rise in warm place until doubled in bulk, about 45 minutes. Punch down bread; spoon into greased 8 x 4 inch loaf pan. Let rise, covered, in warm place for 30 – 40 minutes or until batter rises to edge of pan. Bake at 375 ° for 35 minutes.

HOT MAMA PEPPER JELLY

¾ C sweet red or green bell peppers   ¼ C hot peppers   6 ¼ C sugar   1 ¼ C apple cider vinegar   ¼ C juice from peppers   1 bottle liquid pectin. Remove seeds from the peppers. Coarsely chop peppers, reserve juice. Bring peppers, sugar, vinegar, and pepper juice to a boil. Keep rolling boil for 6 minutes. Remove from heat and add pectin. Boil one minute, stir to mix. Skim off foam. Cool. Rinse glass jars with hot water, dry and add jelly. Seal jars.

ROCK 'EM, SOCK 'EM CARROTS, POTATOES AND MUSHROOMS

2 cans Veg-All, drained   2 cans water-chestnuts, sliced and drained   2/3 C mayonnaise   1 C chopped onion   1 C sliced mushrooms   1 C chopped celery   1 C grated sharp cheese   salt and pepper. Mix ingredients together in casserole dish. Bake 30 minutes at 350°.   Mix 1 C crushed crackers with ¾ C butter; spread on top and bake additional 15 minutes. Hits the spot !

COCKTAIL CAKE

1 C water   1 C sugar   4 eggs   2 C dried fruit   1 t salt   1 C brown sugar   lemon juice   nuts   1 bottle Jack Daniels Black Label Whiskey. Sample the whiskey to check for quality. Take a large bowl from the pantry. Check the whiskey again. To be sure it is the highest quality pour one level cup of whiskey and drink. Repeat this process. Turn on the electric mixer, beat one cup of butter in the large fluffy bowl. Add one teaspoon of sugar and beat again. Make sure the whiskey is still okay. Cry another tup. Turn off the mixer. Beat two leggs and add to the bowl and chuck in the tup of dried fruit. Mix on the turner. If the fried durit get stuck in beaterers, pry it loose with a long drewscriver. Sample the whiskey to check for tonsisticity. Next, sift wor cups of salt or something white. Who really cares. Check the whiskey. Now sift the lemon juice and strain your nuts. Add one table. Spoon something, whatever you have left. Check the whiskey. Grease the oven. Turn the cake tin to 350 ° or in the same direction. Dons forget to beat off the truner. Throw the bowl out the window. Check the whishey again and now off to bed. Canta Sauce is coming.

LC

130

TRAVELIN' BOB

Bob was really a good Travelin Salesman, so good he had several women in every town he traveled to! These 'honeys', as Suitcase Bob fondly called them, would be callin his home at all hours of the day and night. They were just wantin' to know when 'their Bobby was comin to town to see them'. If they caught him at home, they would promise him a GOOD TIME HE WOULD NEVER FORGET!!! If they messed up and called when Sell-Ya-A-Snake Bob was on the road, the Ladies-of-the Night would just hang up on gullible, blonde wife, Tommie, or pretend to have the wrong number.

"Wrong number my booty," Tommie would yell into the phone. After all these years she certainly knew the score, but by darn, she couldn't figure it out! Scrawny Bob was a Travelin Drunk and could barely stay awake after ONE drink of his whiskey! But he could sure make that money! That had to be IT! But, what ever IT was, she vowed with the last phone call to put an end to this travelin circus!

The last night Tommie could ever remember Voyager Bob coming in from the road, he was as drunk as a skunk! He cruised that Big Old Lincoln right across the yard and smashed it into a Big Old Elm tree giving him a real shiner! And Tired-of-IT-All Tommie had a Big Old Surprise just awaitin' for Bob! As he managed to stumble from the vehicle, he strained his blood shot eyes, did a double take, but could barely make out two figures, standing on the porch, throwin' lots of something into the yard!!! As he wobbled closer he thought those 'lots of something' looked an awful lot like HIS CLOTHES! But, who the heck was doing the throwin besides Tommie? As Bob leaned against the nearest tree he sure enough got a good look. "Mama, MAMA, IS THAT YOU?", slurred bewildered Bob. Bob sure did LOVE HIS MAMA!!!

Well, that was the last trip Bob ever made as a travelin' salesman. He got him a sales job in town and except for an occasional fishin' trip, old Bob stuck pretty close to home and made it for dinner every night!

TIP: Watch out! Your Mama can sure make an impact on your life!   PW

RECIPES FOR:

    Suitcase Bob's BlackEyed Pea/Corn Salad   LovinMamas Country Fried Steak 'n Gravy

Goodtime Bobby's Twice Baked Squash   Smashed Sweet Potatoes   Sale-Ya-A-Snake Succotash NoSmores Sundaes

TRAVELIN' BOB

SUITCASE BOB'S BLACK-EYED PEA/CORN SALAD

Combine: 1/3 C Balsamic vinegar   1 T mustard   ¼ C basil/parsley   ½ tsp Kosher salt   ¼ C pepper
     ½ tsp Greek seasonin'   a good shake of garlic powder   Blend in ¼ C Extra Virgin Olive oil
Mix into the dressing: 1 chopped onion   1 10 oz pkg frozen cooked Corn   1 lg can drained /rinsed Black-eyed peas
     ½ cored/seeded/chopped Red Bell pepper/½ Yellow Bell pepper/½ Green pepper   3 stalks chopped celery
          SOUTHERN BOY YUMMY GOOD.....KEEPS BOB AT HOME...THAT NIGHT ANYWAY!!!

LOVIN' MAMAS COUNTRY FRIED STEAK 'N GRAVY

Form a Roux by meltin' ½ C Butter and slowly adding 6 T Flour...whisk together over a low heat...add 2 tsp Salt, 2 tsp Sage,
     2 tsp Hot sauce and 2 ½ C Milk...Simmer until thickens , then just keep warm while you do the rest.
Combine 1 ¼ C flour, 1 T salt/pepper in a shallow dish.....beat 2 eggs and ½ C Buttermilk in another dish......meantime, you are heatin' about an inch of Canola oil in a good ol heavy skillet.
Take about 6 to 8 Beef cutlets...dredge 'em in the dry Flour mixture first...then the Egg mixture...then back into the dry
     flour... carefully place them in the Hot Oil.   FRY for 4 minutes on each side until brown and crispy.
     Reduce heat and slowly add the Roux...Simmer until thoroughly heated.
          BOB CAN EAT NOW.....AND USUALLY BEFORE ANYBODY ELSE!!!

GOODTIME BOBBYS TWICE BAKED SQUASH

Split a large Acorn squash in half lengthwise...slice a small section from the bottom of each half so they sit up like
     little boats. Cook in boilin' water until tender...about 10 minutes. When cooked remove from water...cool...
     and scoop the pulp from the skin.
 Meantime you have crumbled/ browned ½ lb your favorite Sausage in a skillet. Remove some of the fat from the skillet before adding pulp...1 chopped/cored apple...½ tsp salt...¼ tsp nutmeg...¼ tsp cinnamon...1 T brown sugar...Cook 10 minutes.
Place mixture back into the shells...dot with butter and Bake uncovered for about 30 minutes at 350°.

SMASHED SWEET POTATOES

Peel and cut 5 or 6 sweet potatoes in 1 inch cubes. Boil about 15 minutes...drain and return to pan.
     Add: 1 C sour cream   ½ C butter   1 small can chopped green chiles   ¾ tsp salt/¼ tsp pepper...mash...serve hot.

OL BOB ACQUIRED A TASTE FOR THIS SPICY ON HIS TRIPS SOUTH OF THE BORDER!

SALE-YA-A-SNAKE SUCCOTASH
Cook ALL the following together for a GREAT side dish:

1 T olive oil   ¼ tsp red pepper flakes   2 C fresh corn   ½ tsp cumin   ½ tsp chili powder
1 cored/seeded red pepper/1 yellow pepper   1 seeded/chopped jalapeno pepper   1 C drained black beans
1 frozen/cooked baby lima beans   1 small bunch green onion with the greens   1 T lime juice
2 T favorite hot sauce   ¼ C chopped cilantro   2 T chopped chives
GREAT with thick, buttery Mexican Cornbread....purchase 2 pkg. And follow the directions.

NOSMORES SUNDAES
Soften 2 C green Chocolate Mint Ice Cream ice cream......crush 20 thin
chocolate cookie wafers......
Mix these two together in a freezer bowl and freeze until firm.....about 1 hour.
When servin' time, spoon ice cream into bowls and top with:
marshmallow crème   chocolate syrup   broken-up thin mint candy
(for adults only.....2 T Crème de Menthe)
YOU CAN'T RESIST THIS.....JUST LIKE BOB'S LADIES!!!

PW

133

WEDDING BLISS

After years of abuse, of the alcohol persuasion, ones brain just becomes a little pickled! Well, that's what I blamed for THIS desertion anyway! Could it have been the babysitter instead??? Whichever the reason I was left behind this time, who really knows? Bob and I were invited to a beautiful wedding for one of his clients. After eyeballin' every derriere in the crowded church, we headed for the lovely reception.

The feast at this cordial gathering was Elegantly Fabulous! And what a GREAT location, Memphis on the Square! After partaking of delightful hors d'oeuvres and dancing the night away to Disco 70's music, I noticed Bob's Dancin' Fever-Glazed eyes. He was STONED!!! As stoned as the luscious Crab dishes! As marinated as the Fish in Wine Sauce! As creamed as the Smothered Shrimp! Plainly, Bob was as Tipsy as the fruit that enthusiastic guests were downin'.

I looked at PetrifiedBob…..I thought he looked at me…..and then, BOB WAS NO MORE! He turned from my gaze and headed for the outside where many guests were chatterin' empty phrases. I also turned my back, returned to the waiting merrymaking and festive foods, and continued to Trip-the-Night-Fantastic, all the while cheering the happy new couple……."Run for your life…Run for your life!"

As guests began drifting toward waiting carriages I figured I needed to find my periodic-partner Bob. Aimlessly I wandered through the loud, obnoxious remainder, to no avail. Dear Bob had actually spared me embarrassment….. he had NOT become one of the Offensive Ones, at this party anyway! BOB WAS GONE!!!!!

Our parking spot was empty!!! He had forgotten I was one of the twosome…forgotten I was the designated driver…forgotten I was the mother of his two children fast asleep at home with the BABYSITTER!!! Maybe those glazed-over eyes were just HOT with a MINOR Fever!!!!!

TIP: Remember to take your own ride to ANY party where Intoxicated Food is served. Always get a Granny to baby sit! PW

RECIPES FOR:

Glazed-Over Amaretto Baby Ribs   Cognac/Onion Beef Fillets pieces in Pastry
Vodka SpinyPenne Pasta   Drunken Smothered Cheese Shrimp

Smoked BobBQued Oysters   Sherried Avocado Crab Dip

Topped Off Crab/Lobster Sun-dried Tomato Polenta Rounds
Liquored-Up Bacon-Wrapped Scallops

After Dinner Glazed Fruit Tarts
Trip-the-Night-Fantastic Bananas Flambe'
Cheers-for-the Miniature Wedding Cakes

PetrifiedBob's Flowing Champagne Punch

PW

WEDDING BLISS

GLAZED-OVER AMARETTO BABY RIBS
Parboil 3 racks baby-back ribs for 40 minutes to release some of the fat.....While boilin... mix the following:
    1 C Amaretto liqueur   1 C heavy peach syrup   ½ C molasses   ½ C chili sauce
    2 T Worcestershire   2 T Steak sauce   1 tsp garlic powder
Place ribs on paper towel to cool.....after coolin', cut into small pieces for easy eatin' handling.....place on a large
oven pan and cover with sauce.....lay peach slices or halves onto the meat.....cook slowly at 325° ('bout an hour or so)
until the sauce becomes a sticky glaze over the meat.   DELICIOUS!

COGNAC/ONION BEEF FILLETS PIECES IN PASTRY
Brown 2 8 oz beef fillets in hot oil with salt/pepper to taste.....Remove from skillet and saute the following
in the drippin's   1 T butter   1 small chopped yellow onion   1 small chopped red onion
    1 bunch chopped green onions   2 minced garlic cloves.....Add ½ C cognac and ¼ C beef broth
Cut fillets into bite -sized pieces.....return to skillet and simmer all together until juices are glazed over the fillets
Cut commercial Phyllo sheets into foldable bite-sized pieces.....brush with butter and spoon a small fillet piece/sauce
onto each.....fold over the meat and brush with butter again.....run into oven at 325° until golden brown

LIQUORED-UP BACON WRAPPED SCALLOPS
Cover 4 lbs rinsed, drained sea scallops with: 3 T lime juice   2 T chopped cilantro   2 minced garlic cloves
    ¼ tsp salt/pepper   dash Hot sauce   ½ C olive oil   Chill for 30 minutes
Microwave 1 lb cut-in-half bacon only until slightly brown   Remove scallops from mixture/drain
Wrap each scallop with a piece of the slightly cooked bacon and secure with a toothpick.
Place the little wrapped babies on an oil-sprayed grate on the grill.....Cover the grill and cook for 3 to 4 minutes
on each side or until the bacon is crispy   WASH YOUR HANDS BOBO AFTER HANDLIN' THAT BACON!

PW

TOPPED OFF CRAB/LOBSTER SUN-DRIED TOMATO POLENTA ROUNDS

For this dish you need to purchase a pkg of the Polenta rounds.....lay them out on an oven pan.....brush with olive oil.....
Toast slightly, then set aside. Mix the following and bake at 350° for 20 minutes: ½ C diced Lobster   ½ C crabmeat
½ C chopped mushrooms   ½ stick butter   1 C Clam Chowder   1 T sherry   ½ C grated cheddar
When cooked and slightly cooled.....place a spoonful on each Polenta round.....top with a little yellow cheese
OR SERVE AS A CASSEROLE OVER RICE.

SMOKED BOBBQUED OYSTERS

In a shallow, greased 2 qt baking dish, make 2 layers of the following: 2 qt drained oysters   ½ tsp salt/pepper
 splashes of Hot sauce   ½ C chopped basil   ½ C chopped shallots   ¼ C Teriyaki sauce   1 T Worcestershire
2 T lemon juice   2 T BBQ sauce   2 C seasoned bread crumbs   1 C melted butter
Bake at 350° for 30 minutes or bubbly....top with thin lemon slices.....can scoop/dip with lg corn chips

VODKA SPINYPENNE PASTA

Prepare 1 lb pkg Penne pasta as directions indicate.....drain/set aside.
Meantime, saute 3 chopped garlic cloves and 1 chopped onion in 2 T butter and 2 T olive oil.....
add ½ tsp crushed red pepper then remove from heat and stir in: 1 C Vodka   1 14 oz can crushed tomatoes
1 T basil   1 T parsley   1 pkg frozen salad shrimp.....simmer 5 minutes
Add 1 C whipping cream and ½ tsp salt stirring often.....simmer 5 minutes.....Stir in the pasta and cook 2 minutes
Sprinkle with ¾ C grated Parmesan cheese and black pepper to taste.....serve immediately

DRUNKEN SMOTHERED CHEESE SHRIMP

Combine all the following: 1 lg bag of cooked shrimp (cut each shrimp in half)   ¾ C mayonnaise   1 C chopped celery
 1 chopped green pepper   1 chopped medium onion   3 beaten eggs   2 C Herb stuffin mix   1 T garlic/parsley salt
½ C milk   1 C undiluted cream of mushroom soup   1 C undiluted cream of cheddar soup   1 C Sherry
Place in a greased baking dish and bake at 325° for at least 45 minutes.....BUBBLY GOOD over toast rounds.   PW

SHERRIED AVOCADO CRAB DIP

Line a beautiful glass salad bowl with Bibb lettuce.....

Layer the following   6 oz lump crab meat   1 can drained Mandarin orange slices   2 Avocados thinly sliced
    over the lettuce: 1 bottle of drained pink grapefruit sections   1 C chopped walnuts or pecans

Combine the following and pour over the layers: $\frac{1}{2}$ C mayonnaise   2 T catsup   3 to 5 drops Hot sauce
                                        $\frac{1}{4}$ C sherry   1 T garlic powder   3 to 5 drops Worcestershire

SO LUMPY GOOD!   Serve with those lil chicken biscuit crackers or sesame/wheat cracker rounds

TRIP-THE-NIGHT-FANTASTIC BANANAS FLAMBE'

Melt 2 T brown sugar and 1 T butter in a low pretty skillet.....add 1 ripe peeled, length-wise sliced banana and

Sauté until tender.....sprinkle with 1 tsp cinnamon.....Pour $\frac{1}{2}$ oz banana liqueur and 1 oz white rum over the bananas

and FLAME.....being very careful, baste the bananas with the liquid until the flame goes out.....

DON'T LET BOB GET TOO CLOSE...HE MIGHT IGNITE TOO!   Serve immediately over mounds of Ice Cream   WOW!!!

AFTER DINNER GLAZED FRUIT TARTS

Whisk together: 8 egg yolks $\frac{1}{2}$ C sugar $\frac{1}{2}$ C Tequila   1 tsp vanilla.....cook over a low heat, stirring constantly,
                           about 10 min.   Do not boil.....chill the custard about 30 minutes

Fold 1 C heavy whipped cream gently into the chilled mixture.....

Arrange a combination of small strawberries, raspberries, blueberries in small baked pastry tarts.....

Top with tequila cream and garnish with a chocolate mint sprig   YUMMY!

CHEERS FOR THE MINATURE WEDDING CAKES

Have your local bakery make individual guest cakes that are 3 tiers: 1 layer a moist banana cake   1 layer a strawberry
                                                another layer a vanilla

Tint the icing whatever the POOR, POOR Brides colors and top with beautiful icing flowers or tiny fresh flowers that have been dipped to stay fresh....Gardenias would be MARVELOUS!   GRIT YOUR TEETH WHEN YOU CHEER THE COUPLE!

PW

WE'RE BUSTED

Once a month King Robert tortured me with the Bank Statement…..all I needed was a blindfold and last smoke to complete the picture. The condemned person…ME…would march slowly and cautiously upstairs where the Inquisition began. My shell-shocked little children would run-for-the-hills knowing that a certifiable maniac would soon be unleashing his nasty, nefarious tongue! Bad Bob, The Bean Counter, should have been a Hatchet Man for the Mob!

Bobby Big Mouth was as 'tight as bark on a tree' and as mean as a' Junkyard Dog.' He would go over every sales slip from toilet paper to baby aspirin, yelling, "We're Busted!" I usually sat staring at the checkbook like a zombie for about thirty minutes or so, or until I finally flipped my lid and told Bob just where he could stick his receipts! Funny, but he never really appreciated my opinion!

However, I did get a small amount of pleasure by preparing NOTHING but Chicken for the next two weeks. I did learn something from this Fiasco…..how to cook chicken 365 different ways. Bob started to crow like a Rooster around day six and it was invigorating! He always thought he Ruled the Roost anyway!!!

TIP: What goes around comes around, usually two-fowl…..I mean two-fold!

RECIPES FOR:

Brazen White Wine Chicken   Stuff-It Chicken Casserole   Stick It! Chicken Squares
              Hit Man Garlicky Chicken   Moxie Marinated Chicken
              Supreme Jerk Chicken   Nutty Spiced Chicken

LC

WE'RE BUSTED

BRAZEN WHITE WINE CHICKEN

1 whole chicken   1 C dry white wine   1 T lemon juice   ½ t paprika   ¼ C butter   ¼ C chopped onion   3 t salt   ¼ C chopped parsley   ¼ t pepper. Mix and pour over chicken. Bake 1 ½ hours at 350°. BUY AN EXTRA BOTTLE OF WINE, YOU MAY NEED IT !

STUFF-IT CHICKEN CASSEROLE

1 (8 oz) package herb seasoned stuffing   3 C cubed, cooked or canned chicken   ½ C butter   ½ C flour   ¼ t salt   Dash pepper   4 C chicken broth   6 eggs slightly beaten   Pimiento mushroom sauce. Prepare stuffing according to package for dry stuffing. Layer stuffing   in 13 x 9 x 2 in baking dish; top with chicken. In large saucepan, melt butter; blend in flour and seasonings. Add broth, cook and stir until mixture thickens. Stir small amount of hot mix into eggs, add hot mix slowly, stirring well, pour over chicken. Bake at 325 ° 40 – 45 minutes. Serve with Pimiento-Mushroom sauce: 1 can cream of mushroom soup   ¼ C milk   1 C sour cream   ¼ C pimiento. Mix together, heat and stir until hot. BOB THE BEAN COUNTER FLIPPED OUT WHILE STUFFIN HIS FOWL MOUTH !

STICK IT! CHICKEN SQUARES

3 C cooked chicken   1 ½ C celery chopped   1 C mayonnaise   1 can mushroom soup   2 C cooked rice   1 ½ T lemon juice   1 ½ T minced onion   salt and pepper   cracker crumbs. Skin and bone the chicken and cut into small pieces. Add celery, mayonnaise, mushroom soup, rice, lemon juice, onion, salt and pepper. Mix well and spread into 12 x 8 inch greased baking dish. Sprinkle cracker crumbs on top and bake 30 minutes at 350°. YOU KNOW WHERE I TOLD EL CHEAPO TO STICK IT !

HIT MAN GARLICKY CHICKEN

2 (10 oz) packages frozen chopped spinach   6 chicken breast halves, skinned   15 garlic cloves, unpeeled   1 can cream of chicken soup   1 ½ C dry white wine   6 garlic cloves, peeled   1 t ground ginger   6 (1-oz) slices Swiss cheese   4 green onions, chopped. Thaw and drain spinach. Place chicken in lightly greased 13 x 9 x 2 inch baking dish. Arrange unpeeled garlic around chicken; spread spinach and chopped onion over top of chicken. Combine soup, wine, peeled garlic cloves and ginger in blender and process until smooth. Pour over chicken. Cover and take 1 hour at 350°. Top with cheese and bake uncovered additional 5 minutes. VAMPIRES WILL NOT GET YOU WHEN YOU EAT THIS GARLIC DELIGHT !

MOXIE MARINATED CHICKEN

1 16 oz bag of bowtie pasta   4-6 chicken breasts   1 can sliced black olives drained   ½ C sun-dried tomatoes   ½ C chopped purple onion   1 block (8 oz) fete cheese   1 large bottle zesty Italian dressing. Cook pasta according to package directions. Cook chicken and shred. Combine all ingredients and refrigerate over night. THIS IS A HIT BELOW THE BELT !

SUPREME JERK CHICKEN

3 lbs chicken   6 T Jerk seasoning   butter or vegetable oil. Rub the chicken with butter or vegetable oil. Sprinkle with jerk seasoning and rub in well. Let it set for at least one hour. Grill on the barbeque and add more seasoning for additional spice! BOB WOULD START TO CROW! AIN'T NOTHIN' CROWIN' BUT THE ROOSTER IN THE PEN AND HE WOULDN'T BE CROWIN' IF IT WASN'T FOR THE HEN !

NUTTY SPICED CHICKEN

½ t finely shredded lime peel   1/3 C lime juice   2 T cooking oil   1 t crushed dried thyme   1 t cracked black pepper   ½ t garlic salt   ½ C crushed pecans   2 – 2 ½ lbs chicken, cut up. Mix together lime peel, lime juice, cooking oil, thyme, pepper, garlic salt and pecans. Place chicken, skin side down, on broiler pan. Cover chicken with half of sauce. Broil 15 – 18 minutes, brushing often with remaining sauce. Turn chicken over, add remaining sauce. Broil an additional 10 – 15 minutes or until pinkness is gone. NUTTER NUTTY CHICKEN FOR THE NUTSO !

LC

WINE, ROSES, AND SOUP

EllaRuth knew she had met her Soul Mate when Sporty Bob came along. He just couldn't leave her side! He wined her, he dined her, and he gave her beautiful roses at least once or twice a month. These were big bunches that meant to EllaRuth that their love was really growing into a full-blown romance! What really turned EllaRuth on was this Big Ski boat Bob owned. The thing would turn into a fishin boat on a whim!

Ellie and Bobbie would join all his friends at the Lake and boat all day long. The lake fun would always begin and end at a place his gang fondly called, Beer Beach. EllaRuth and her bikini were always invited to ride in the boat and let her pretty long blonde hair flow in the cheerful air of Beer Beach, while the wives and kiddies of his friends played in the waters of Beer Beach. She really didn't take notice of THIS cause she was In Love and having THE MOST Spectacular Time of her life!

By the end of summer Bobby had proposed to EllaRuth and she couldn't have been more elated. The frequent gifts, flowers, and constant fun had won her over...the wedding was to be in the Fall of that same year. When they weren't out having the time of their lives, or Sporty Bob was fishing with his Buddies, (they particularly liked night fishin even when it was really chilly) EllaRuth was cookin' for her man. Bob really liked her Homemade Soups and always managed to be there when she created these Hot Delights and Special Breads or Sandwiches.

Well, their Special Day arrived and Bob just had to have every last one of his Best Buddies in the Wedding. With all the merrymaking you would have thought Bob was marrying each of them! Their Honeymoon was a trip to the mountains for an Oktoberfest with, of course, all his friends, their wives, and children. SauerBob spent his nights drinkin' beer with his KrautBuddies. EllaRuth would just sit around the warm fires, share recipes, and listen to children scream at one another. All those beautiful nighties stayed in her suitcase and she would don a borrowed flannel Granny Gown from one of the wives. Why not keep herself warm.....Bob never came in until right before sunrise and slept most of the day.

During the day, Ella visited the Sights with the female group who was constantly refereeing the kids! What a lovely time she was having on HER Honeymoon!!! That old sayin' about Love Being Lovelier the Second Time Around certainly fell short with this situation! Bob never laid a hand on her during THEIR Honeymoon and never spent any time alone with her. This was SOME TIME WONDERFUL to remember.....if you were Looney Tunes!!!

As Fall turned to Winter, they ate more soup and great breads, rarely had conversation, and even more rarely had sex or even a hint of the good old times. She only had her memories of when Bobbie couldn't keep his hands off her. She also had memories of gifts and roses and fine wine. She also had the memories of her Honeymoon spent with Bob's Buddies wives and children!

As Winter turned to Spring the fishin began, particularly those Night Fishin' trips when no catch was EVER brought home! With early Summer, ski time arrived and they'd meet the Buddies and their wives and kids at Beer Beach. But this Summer, EllaRuth didn't get to go out in the boat and let her new short blonde hair bobble in the breeze. She was now One-of-the Lonely playing in the waters of Beer Beach! This Summer EllaRuth DID take notice of THIS because she was no longer IN LOVE, and she was certainly having THE WORST TIME of her life! What is it they say about the Third Time Around?????

TIP: Life is Lovelier when you learn To Love Yourself, Be with Yourself, and Take Care of Yourself!!!
        Take heed ladies......Night Fishin is a RUSE!!!!!

RECIPES FOR:

HONEYMOON HELL! Oktoberfest Sandwich   Bikini MozzarElla Panini
                Night Fishin Mystery Chowder
                    Beer Beach Muffins

PW

WINE, ROSES, AND SOUP

BIKINI mozzarELLA PANINI
Slice 1 loaf of fresh Italian hard crust bread lengthwise then into 6 individual pieces.
Rub the inside of each piece with garlic......Drizzle each piece with olive oil, salt/pepper/garlic salt.....Layer each with
 Mozzarella slices...tomato slices...fresh basil leaves.....butter the outside of each bread.....cook/grill in a hot iron
skillet til brown and melty....serve warm   WOULD BE GREAT WITH AN ICE COLD BEER...RIGHT BOB?

HONEYMOON HELL! OKTOBERFEST SANDWICH
Split 1 20 oz pkg Hot Bratwurst (each piece) $\frac{1}{2}$ way through lengthwise.....flatten each piece then cook accordin'
to the pkg.....remove and set aside.....to the skillet add: 1 C sliced red onion $\frac{1}{2}$ C sliced green onions including greens
          1 15 oz drained sauerkraut $\frac{3}{4}$ tsp sugar $\frac{3}{4}$ garlic powder   4 dashes Hot sauce   Saute about 5 or minutes
then put the bratwurst back into the skillet with the mixture and cook until hot and how you like it.....
Meantime, place a slice of Swiss cheese on each needed Hoagie buns with a smear of brown mustard and favorite relish.....
Spoon the mixture onto each Hoagie and you have THE BEST SANDWICH EVER...BET BOB LOVES 'EM!

NIGHT FISHIN MYSTERY CHOWDER
Mix ALL these ingredients together in a Dutch oven...bring to a boil...reduce heat/simmer about 1 hour:
2 lb browned pork Sausage   4 C water   1 16 oz can kidney Beans   1 16 oz can black Beans   2 16 oz cans stewed
tomatoes   1 16 oz can white beans   2 chopped medium onions   2 peeled, diced potatoes $\frac{1}{2}$ C uncooked Brown rice
$\frac{1}{2}$ pkg chili mix   1 tsp garlic salt $\frac{1}{2}$ tsp thyme/basil/pepper   1 lg bay leaf   (all cans of whatever are dumped in
with juices)

BOB WON'T BE ABLE TO WAIT UNTIL IT'S READY!

BEER BEACH MUFFINS
Thoroughly mix the following then bake in well-buttered muffin tins at 350° for about 20 minutes:
     4 C powdered biscuit mix   1 12 oz can beer   3 T sugar $\frac{1}{2}$ C cheddar cheese   1 T chopped chives
PW

YUM YUM BLACKBERRY PIE

On a cold morning in January as Bob was about to leave for the office, Annabeth called to him asking, "Whatcha want for dinner tonight?" Through all the years of lies and deceit, Annabeth still believed what her Mama always told her…."Annabeth, if you want to keep your husband at home…fix him a good dinner every night." Well, Annabeth wasn't absolutely sure Mama knew what she was talkin about since she wasn't married to a Dyed-in-the-WOOL Bob! But faithful Annabeth was gonna keep the faith for another night anyway!

Bob hesitated but finally responded with, "How about that great crusty Fish you make and one of those Blackberry Pies…yea, that's what I want." "Sounds good to me too," Annabeth called back. " See ya tonight." Annabeth spent the entire afternoon in preparation of Bob's favorite meal, missing her workout at the Gym and her Garden Club meeting. She figured that trying to mend a broken marriage was more important sometimes than what she wanted to do for herself. Hadn't worked yet, but you have to have a little hope, or so she thought at the time!

Six o'clock came and went and so did three and four and five more hours. Finally she gave up the hope and figured Bob was with Hope somewhere, eatin something! She placed a plate of the luscious dinner in the still warm oven along with the beautiful purple dessert and wearily went to bed. She left the oven light on for a cue to the food just in case he came in. "What a good dummy wife you are," Annabeth quietly spoke to her Blonde self.

The next morning she awoke to the sound of a car pulling into the drive. Reluctantly, Annabeth walked downstairs, flicked off the oven runway light and waited. As Bob walked in the faint aroma of last nights dinner still hung in the frozen air.

He gulped, knowing he better come with something quick in order to get the upper hand. Without a word, Bob walked to the table, sat down, unfolded the napkin, picked up the waiting fork and knife, and demandingly said, "Where's that great Fish and Blackberry Pie I ordered yesterday."

Annabeth silently walked to the oven and pulled out that luscious but dry, stone cold dinner, with its purple dessert and politely, as a good Southern woman would do, dumped it in Bob's lap!!!!!

PW

TIP: Never believe your mama…..go with your gut feeling!!!
      Always make sure your dinners have beautiful, rich, bright, staining color…..you never know when you
      might be decorating with 'em!   Cooking Oil or Butter works good too!!!

RECIPES FOR:

Screwin' Hope n Ginger/Orange Drivers

Southern Woman Crusted Tilapia topped with They Were Crispy! Onion Rings
Last Time Fried Okra   See Ya Tonight? Potato/Squash Croquettes
Hadn't Worked Yet Cornbread Bites

Dumpin' Bob's Yummy Blackberry Pie
Doubtin' Mama Homemade Fresh Blueberry Ice Cream

PW

147

YUM YUM BLACKBERRY PIE

SOUTHERN WOMAN CRUSTED TILAPIA
Combine ¼ C finely chopped almonds with ¼ C flour in
a shallow bowl.....dredge 4 6 oz tilapia fillets in the
Almond mixture.....melt 2 T butter with 2 T olive oil
in a heavy skillet over medium heat.....cook 4 minutes
On each side.....remove and move to a platter.....add the
Remaining flour/almond mixture to the skillet .....cook
And stir constantly.....spoon the mixture over the fish.
OUT OF SIGHT!!! Top with onion rings.

THEY WERE CRISPY! ONION RINGS
Cut 1 large onion into ¼ inch slices.....separate into
rings. Beat ¼ can Beer....¼ Buttermilk....1 egg.
Dredge rings in ½ C flour then into the batter,
then back into the flour.....cook in a thin layer of
oil in a skillet for just a minute.....Place the rings
on an oil coated bakin' sheet and bake at 400° for 3
or 4 minutes.....sprinkle with salt and EAT!
Repeat process until all rings are cooked.

LAST TIME FRIED OKRA
Mix 1 C cornmeal with ½ C flour and ½ tsp salt.....Let 1 10 oz box frozen okra thawed.....drench the lil pieces in the flour
mixture, Let sit at least 1 hour.....Heat 1 inch of oil in a heavy skillet.....when its hot, Cook a few okra at a time so as not to
overcrowd...   Overcrowdin' presents problems..... JUST LIKE IT DOES WITH BOB...
THINGS TEND TO OVERLAP ONE ANOTHER IN A BIG GROUP...IF YOU GET MY DRIFT!!!.....
Back to the lil okra...cook about 5 minutes on each side. Drain and eat 'em up!!!! Great with ketchup.

SEE YA TONIGHT? POTATO/SQUASH CROQUETTES
Finely chop all together: 1 C cubed red potatoes   1 C cubed squash   1 C onion   Dump into a bowl and stir in
1 egg   about 8 T flour   1 tsp salt   2 tsp pepper   Drop by large spoonfuls into the HOT oil. Drain on paper towel.

THIS IS ALL TOO GOOD FOR THAT MAN TO MISS.....BUT I BETCHA HE DOES!   PW

HADN'T WORKED YET CORNBREAD STICKS

Mix together: 1 cup yellow cornmeal   ½ C flour   1 tsp salt/pepper   ¼ tsp baking soda
Stir into the mixture: 1 ¼ C buttermilk ¼ C softened butter   1 lg egg
Heat a cornstick pan in a 450° oven for a few minutes...plop a little oil in each pan then the batter.
Bake at 450 for about 18 to 20 minutes or until golden brown.
    OH, SO GOOD...I NEED TO EAT ONE RIGHT NOW WITH LOTS OF BUTTER! CANT WAIT FOR BOB...

DUMPIN BOB'S YUMMY BLACKBERRY PIE

Mix together: 1 ¼ C sugar   ¼ C flour   1/8 tsp salt
Add this mixture to 4 C fresh blackberries.....toss to coat every little joker...you want every one to get SOME SUGAR!
Pour these lil sugar into a prepared 9 inch pie crust.....top with another 9 inch crust...sealing and crimping the edges
Carefully cover the edges with foil and bake at 375° for 25 to 30 minutes.....unfoil the edges and bake about
25 more minutes or till golden brown.....HONESTLY...YOU WILL NOT BELIEVE THIS ONE...WATCH THE STAINING!
Cover the slightly warm pie with the AWESOME Homemade Ice Cream...BOB IS MISSIN OUT.....OH SHUCKS!

DOUBTIN MAMA HOMEMADE FRESH BLUE BERRY ICE CREAM

Cream 2 C sugar with 4 eggs   Add a dash of salt and 1 tsp vanilla   Pour the mixture into your ice cream freezer
Container....throw in 1 to 2 C fresh blueberries   GREAT if you could PICK the berries...you really appreciate the
Wonderful darlin's much more.....AND I KNOW YOU HAVE TIME ON YOUR HANDS IF YOU'RE MARRIED TO BOB!!!
PW

LIBATION RECIPES

BABY BLUE MARGARITA
Mix 1 can frozen Margarita Mix with 1 can Tequila,
½ can Blue Curacao, ½ can Lime juice, and a
Splash of orange liqueur.   WATCH OUT!!!

MARY LOU'S BEFORE DINNER RED PICK-ME-UPS
Puree 1 10 oz box Strawberries. Pour into a pitcher.
Blender 3 C ice with 1 C frozen Blueberries, 1 ripe
Banana, ¾ C Vodka, ½ C Pineapple juice, ½ C Cranberry
juice, and ½ C Crème de Coconut. Mix with pureed
Strawberries and COOL YOURSELF DOWN, MAMA!!!

BOBACLAUS PEPPERMINT EGGNOG
  DELICIOUS WITH OR WITHOUT THE NOG!!!
Mix all the following together in a punch bowl:
1 pint scoops of Pink Peppermint Ice Cream
2 C prepared Dairy Eggnog   1 C Heavy whipped Cream
½ C crushed peppermint sticks   1 large bottle of
chilled Club Soda   1 C Whiskey   BEAUTIFUL!

BUSHY TREE SOURS
In a NEATO pitcher, add 1 bottle Dry Sherry to 1 6 oz
Can frozen Pink Lemonade. Refrigerate overnight.....Serve over crushed Ice. STUNNING LIL YUM YUM!!!

BEST BUDDIES STINGER
1 oz Scotch   ½ ox white crème de menthe

PARTEE CHAMPAGNE PUNCH
In a cool punch bowl, Mix 1 ½ C powdered sugar
   with ½ C Curacao well. Stir in ½ C Cognac and
½ C Maraschino cherry juice. MIX WELL LIKE
BOB DOES WITH ALL THE FEMALE GUESTS!!
Place a 1 quart block of Pineapple Sherbet in the
center of the bowl. SLOWLY add 3 bottles cold
Champagne, 1 thinly sliced Orange and 1 thinly
sliced Lemon. COUNT ON REFILLS...YUMMY!!!

RED-NOSED DADO FRUIT PUNCH
GOOD WITH OR WITHOUT THE RED NOSE.....
      IF YOU KNOW WHAT I MEAN!
In a punch bowl, dissolve 1 C sugar in 4 qt water.
   Add and Mix well: 2 6 oz frozen orange juice
      1 6 oz lemonade   1 lg frozen pineapple juice
1 L Icy Cold Ginger Ale   1 lg can Vodka or Rum
      ALWAYS A HIT JUST LIKE BOB!!!

PW

SUGAR DRIPPIN MELON COOLER

Place 4 C seedless Watermelon in the freezer
For 4 hrs. Dip cocktail glass rims in Lime juice
then Sugar. Process the frozen watermelon,
½ C Tequila, ¼ C sugar, 1 T lime rind, ¼ C lime.
2 T chocolate or regular Mint leaves. Carefully
Pour into rimmed glasses…Top with a sprig of Mint.

BOB THINGS

Combine…cover…shake…chill and pour into a Chilly
Martini glass:
2 C ice cubes   ¼ C orange juice   ¼ C vodka
2 T orange liqueur. Float a sprig of mint in each glass
   or a very thin slice of orange. WOW WHEW!!!

SHAKENUP BOBITINI

Combine ¼ C Pear Vodka…..2 T Pear Liqueur…..
2 T Lemon juice…..2 T simple sugar. SHAKE!
SHAKE! SHAKE! Pour into a Martini glass and float
a thin slice of fresh Pear. HEAVENLY!

PUNCHBOWL SCORPIONS

Mix ALL the following together in a blender with 1 C chopped ice: 8 oz Rum   8 oz fresh orange juice   1 ½ oz Gin
   5 oz. Fresh squeezed lemon juice   1 ½ oz Brandy   3 oz Orgeat syrup   Pour into a bowl filled with chopped ice.
Float some pretty flowers in this concoction. GUARANTEED TO KNOCK BOB OUT TO THE STARS!!! YES INDEED!!!

PW

SMOOTH PYTHON

Mix…Chill…Serve with an orange slice and a
Pineapple Chunk:
   1 oz Rum   1 oz Bourbon
1 ½ tsp powdered sugar   1 oz lemon juice
     2 oz orange/pineapple/mango juice
      THIS IS BOB'S SWAMP DRINK!

SCARLET HARLOTS

Place a brown sugar cube in each
Champagne glass…..
Pour 2 T Pomegranate OR Cranberry juice and
½ C Champagne over the cube.
Serve NOW! Can use a regular sugar cube.

SWINGIN' DOOR THINGS

Mix and stir…..1 oz Coffee Liqueur…..
2 oz Raspberry Vodka…..½ C Soda.
Pour over ice and add a slice of fresh Lime.
A KNOCKOUT!

JENNIBLUES
Mix all together with chopped ice:
1 ½ oz favorite Whiskey
¾ oz Blueberry Schnapps
4 oz Sweet/Sour Mix
3 oz Lemon-Lime Soda

SEEING RED SANGRIA
In a large bowl add: 1 unpeeled, seeded/sliced orange
   1 unpeeled seeded/sliced lemon   a handful Strawberries
   A handful Blueberries   1 peeled/sliced Peach
   2 tsp Sugar   1 oz favorite fruit-flavored liqueur
   1 oz Brandy   Let stand at room temperature for
   Several hours. Add 1 bottle Red Dry Wine and LOTS
   of chopped ice. Stir with a wooden spoon...QUAINT!!!

HONEYDIDDEW COOLERS
Place 8 C Honeydew Melon cubes in the freezer....freeze 8 hours.
In a blender blend 1 cup Vodka   1 6 oz can frozen lemonade or
Limeade   2 C Ginger Ale   ½ C crushed ice and the melon.
Pour into a glass pitcher and immediately serve. SO COOL!
  JUST AS GREAT WITHOUT THE VODKA...BUT NOT BOB'S!

DEEP SOUTH COFFEE
Mix: 1 oz Coffee Liqueur
   ½ oz Crème de Cacao
   1 oz Vanilla Vodka
Place in lil cream pitchers
   to pour into cups of coffee
QUITE SOUTHERN INDEED!

NO SEX ON THE BEACH
Mix ALL together:
   1 oz Vodka
   ½ oz Melon Liqueur
   ½ oz Peach Schnapps
   1 ¾ oz Orange juice
   1 ¾ oz Cranberry juice
   1 ¾ oz Pineapple juice
   ½ oz Raspberry Liqueur
Pour over lots of crushed ice
and THIS IS THE REASON
YOU PROBABLY WILL NOT
HAVE   SEX
            ON THE
            BEACH......
FANTASTIC, BUT A PASSER-OUTTER!!!

TO DIE FOR MELON COOLERS
Mix together: 1 oz Melon Liqueur
   1 oz Apricot Schnapps
   1 6 oz frozen Pineapple juice
   2 C Lemon/Lime Soda
   1 T Grenadine
Pour over lots of crushed and
add a skewer of lil fruits.

PW

FLIRTATIOUS FLITINIS
Mix the following: shake with ice....and pour into a Martini glass rimmed with a wedge of Tangerine, then dipped
2 oz Orange Vodka   in sugar.
¼ oz Campari
1 oz Pomegranate juice
Juice of ½ Tangerine   SOMETHING DIFFERENT, JUST LIKE BOB LIKES!

RUMMY BOB COCKTAILS
Combine ALL ingredients in a pitcher. Pour over crushed ice with a slice of lime.   DANCE KING COFFEE
¾ C Amber Rum   ½ C Coconut Rum   ¼ C Apricot BrandyMix   1 oz Coffee Liqueur
1 C Pineapple juice   ¾ C Orange juice   ¼ C Pink Grapefruit juice   2 oz Vodka
BOB'S FAVORITE PARTICULARLY WHEN WEARIN' THOSE WHITE SHOES   1 oz Milk
                                                                                      Mix vigorously

SNAKES-IN-THE-GRASS   ## BEASTY BOBS   Pour over ice.
1 oz Green Creme de Menthe   l oz Scotch   WAKES BOB UP.... THEN PUTS HIM
1 oz white creme de cacao   ½ oz sweet Vermouth   BACK TO SLEEP! YES!!!
1 T Cream   Lemon peel
Shake/ Pour over crushed ice.   Orange peel Pour over crushed ice after twistin' the fruit.
You'll slither for more!

SHENANIGAN MY ASS AGAIN MANGO BONGOS
Mix together in a large pitcher of crushed ice:
2 C Passion-fruit juice 1 C blended Mangos / Crushed Pineapples 2 C Orange juice
1 C Cranberry juice   ½ C Pineapple Juice   ½ C Apple juice   1 C Coconut Rum Stir well. FABULOUS!!!

BLOODY JACKABOBS
Mix together in a pitcher of crushed ice: 6 oz Tomato or V-8 Juice   6 oz Vodka   juice of 2 lemons
1 ½ T Worcestershire sauce 1 tsp celery salt 1 ½ tsp pepper juice of 1 lime Stir with celery stalk. WOW!!   PW

RAINBOW MANGO MARGARITA

2 oz Mango Vodka   1 ½ C Pomegranate juice   1 oz Sweet/Sour Mix ½ oz Triple Sec 1 oz fresh Lime Shake well with ice and pour into a chilled glass....rimmed with lime and sugar.
A DIFFERENT MARGARITA .... BUT SOMETIMES YOU NEED A CHANGE AFTER DEALIN' WITH BOB.

FRENCH PEACH FIZZ

Fill a shaker with crushed ice and several Mint leaves. Pour 1 ½ oz Peach Vodka   ¾ oz Simple Sugar
                        ¾ oz fresh lime juice   dash of bitters   2 oz chilled Soda water and
shake vigorously. Pour into a stubby glass of ice with a slice of fresh peach and a Mint sprig. PERFECT!

PETRIFIED BOB'S FLOWING CHAMPAGNE PUNCH

Mix all together in a punchbowl: 46 oz can cold Pineapple juice 3 C Orange juice 2 C Cranberry juice
                    2 C Guava juice   ¾ C powdered sugar ¼ C Lime juice
When ready to serve pour 2 to 3 bottles of very cold Champagne into the mix. Float a frozen fruited ice ring
In this LUSCIOUS, BUBBLY CHEER. THEY'LL BE HOLLERIN' FOR MORE!!!

NIGHT FISHIN' JIGGLERS

This GOSH ALL MIGHTY MIXTURE needs to be combined in a large container that can be refrigerated.
            2 Liter Bourbon   ½ Liter Dark Rum   1 ¼ C sugar   7 C strong brewed Tea
            3 ½ cups fresh Lemon juice   2 QT Orange juice   1 QT Pineapple juice
Mix and refrigerate for 2 to 3 days. THOSE GOOD OL' NIGHT FISHIN' GUYS CARRY THIS IN THEIR THERMOS.
WELL, BOB DOES ANY WAY....AND HIS BUDDIES!!! DO YA REALLY BELIEVE THEY'RE FISHIN' AT NIGHT?????

SCREWIN' HOPE 'N' GINGER/ORANGE DRIVERS

Freeze 8 C Cantaloupe for several hours. Plop 'em into the blender with 2 tsp. fresh Ginger 1 C Banana Rum
¼ C fresh Lime juice ¼ sugar 2 T Mint leaves. Blend until slushy. Drink and HOPE YOU DON'T HAVE TO SEE BOB!!!

INDEX

APPETIZERS

SALADS

VEGETABLES

MAIN DISHES

PIZZA, SOUPS, SANDWICHES, AND BURGERS

Daddy BobO Burgers 20
MuscleHead Mussel Chowder 23
Extra Innings Leftover Simpleton Meatloaf Sandwich 32
Nerd Nacho Grande   113
Honeymoon Hell! Oktoberfest Sandwich 145
Bikini MozzarElla Panini 145
Hide-the-Winnie Hotdogs 113
Hound Dogs in Crescent Rolls 56

Double Whammy on Rye 113
MeatHead Meatball Subs 113
In the Sack Mushroom Pizza 93
Night Fishin Mystery Chowder 145
Dork Burgers   113
Play Doctor Cheesy Pizza 93
Mess Around Meaty Pizza 93

BREADS

Crusty Loaf Bread with Virgin Olive Oil 13
Sneaky Pete Cornbread 116
Out-of-Towner Grilled Garlic Bread 62
Extra Inning/Extra Whammy Muffins 30
Heavenly Bread 129
Hothead Biscuits with Sausage Gravy 39
Tummy Pleasin' French Toast with Berries 38
Peanut Butter and BoBanana Sandwiches 56

Hushpuppy Ho' Balls 101
Early Rising Rolls   27
Beer Joint Muffins 127
Beer Beach Muffins 145
Dirty Garlic Bread 82
Infatuating Jelly Donuts 56
Hadn't Worked Yet Cornbread Bites 149

DESSERTS

Italian Stallion Crème Cake 14

Stingy Tingly Key Lime Tarts 18

Blue Ice Cream 21

Black Lace Cookies   28

Homerun Stretch Ice Cream Crepes 32

Ugly Ducklin' Cake 43

Spirit-Filled Hint-of-Mint Caramel Brownies 47

Moon You Pie 52

Holy Terror Pie 52

Fudge You Pie 53

Copperhead Cookies 57

Dusty BillieBob Brownies 62

FABULOUS Magnolia Chocolate Delight 66

Moonin' Booty Bars 75

Pale Blonde Brownies 75

Warm Apple Cake 82

Way Down Deep Peach Cobbler 86

Out-Like-A-Light Burgundy Pie   97

Out of the Ordinary Pound! Pound! Cake 102

This or That Places Lemony Cheesecake Pie 109

Pioneer Puddin Tarts 124

Cocktail Cake 130

After Dinner Glazed Fruit Tarts 138

Cheers-for-the Minature Wedding Cakes 138

Grasshopper Pie 18

Fuzzy White Coconut Cake 21

Sexy Red Velvet Cake   46

Red/Green Jello Delight 46

Quick Pale Blonde Brownies   36

Red Devil Cake 43

Blonde Flan 50

Plastered Pumpkin Pie 52

Nuts to You Pie 53

GI Blue Shimmying Jello in Cantaloupe halves 56

Sweet 'n Gooey Red Viper Ice Cream 57

Hoppin Mad Pie 53

Raisin Hell Nut Pie/Homemade Ice Cream 69

SouthernBoy Getcha Cookies 74

Sinsational Devils Food Cake 90

Dumpin Bob's Yummy Blackberry Pie 149

Splashin' Siblings Homemade Strawberry Ice Cream   90

LaLa Land Double Chocolate Cheesecake 98

Strawberry Afternoon Delight 115

Salted NutNut-Head Cake 120

Banana Split-Your-Pants Pie 124

NoSmores Sundaes 133

Trip-the-Night-Fantastic Banana Flambe 138

Doubtin Mama Homemade Fresh Blueberry Ice Cream 149

BEVERAGES

Buckets of Licey Icy Fruity Waters 16
Dat Blame Good Sweet Tea   28
Spiced-Up Tea 120
Ready To Drink or Toss Iced Tea   82
Beguiling Peachy Sweet Tea 102
Hot Tub Chocolate 105

Fresh Squeezed Lemonade 21
Bob's Au Lait Café Mix   30
Tickled Pink Lemonade 56
DoGooder Limeade 90
Icy Purple Blush 105
French Peach Fizz 115

BEER

We recommend any and all Domestic and Imported Light and Dark Beers that suit YOUR TASTE.

LIBATIONS
COOL COCKTAILS

Baby Blue Margaritas 150
Bushy Tree Sours   150
Best Buddies Stingers 150
MaryLou's Before Dinner Red Pick-Me-Ups 150
ParTee Champagne Punch 150
BobaClaus Peppermint Eggnog 150
Red-Nosed Dado Fruit Punch 150
Punchbowl Scorpions 151
Sugar-Drippin Melon Coolers   151
Smooth Pythons 151
Bob Things 151
Scarlet Harlots 151
ShakenUp Bobitinis 151
Swingin Door Things 151
Seeing Red Sangria 152
JenniBlues 152

HoneyDidDew Coolers 152
To-Die-For Melon Coolers 152
Flirtatious Flitinis 153
RummyBob Cocktails 153
Snakes-in-the-Grass 153
Dance King Coffee 153
Beastie Bob's 153
Shenanigan My Ass Again Mango Bongos 153
Rainbow Mango Margaritas   154
French Peach Fizz 154
Bloody JackaBobs 153
PetrifiedBobs Flowing Champagne Punch 154
Night Fishin Jigglers 154
Screwin Hope 'n Ginger/Orange Drivers 154
No Sex on the Beach 152

WINES

RED WINES	Rose' Claret Chianti Syrah Burgundy Shiraz Red Bordeaux Zinfandel Pinot Noir Cabernet Sauvignon Merlot Beaujolais Vermouth Port	Slightly Chilled	Serve anytime, with or without food
WHITE WINE	Vermouth Rhine Chablis Sauterne Muscat Riesling Gewurztraminer White Bordeaux Chardonnay Sauvignon Blanc Chenin Blanc Pinot Gris Verdicchio Fume	Chilled	Serve anytime, with or without food
SPARKLING WINE	Champagne Sparkling Burgundy Sparkling Shiraz	Chilled	Serve anytime, with or without food
DESSERT WINE	Port Muscatel Tokay Champagne Sherry Madeira Sauterne Marsala Malaga	Cool Room Temperature	After Dinner With Dessert

BY NO MEANS ARE THESE THE ONLY WINE CHOICES
AS TO THE PAIRING OF WINE WITH FOODS.....USE YOUR GUT FEELIN', YOUR INSTINCTS,
AND BY ALL MEANS, USE YOUR IMAGINATION.....
Taste it over and over again like BOB does!!!

PW

Main Street Publishing, Inc.

206 E. Main Street Suite 207

P.O.Box 696

Jackson, Tn 38301

Toll Free #: 866-457-7379

or

Local #: 731-427-7379

Visit us on the web:

www.mainstreetpublishing.com

www.mspbooks.com

E-Mail: mspsupport@charterinternet.com